MIKE KEARBY

The Road to a Hanging

LEISURE BOOKS NEW YORK CITY

A LEISURE BOOK®

January 2008

Published by

Dorchester Publishing Co., Inc.
200 Madison Avenue
New York, NY 10016

ISBN 10: 0-8439-6022-1
ISBN 13: 978-0-8439-6022-8

Printed in the United States of America.

10 9 8 7 6 5 4 3 2 1

Visit us on the web at www.dorchesterpub.com.

The Road to a Hanging

Prologue

Anderson Farm, Missouri 1864

Wide ribbons of light peered over the horizon, heating a fog that had settled on the hemp fields during the cool of the night. Touched by the sun's warming rays, the scorched mist rose skyward in slender wisps of gray, hanging delicately in the air like a spider's web. The seasonably cool morning temperature gave no hint to the heat of an extended Missouri summer and dangled a deceptive offering to the slaves of Anderson Farm. The slave workers, shackled in perpetual bondage, always included in their prayers the hope of a temperate day in which to toil.

George Washington Anderson looked to the east and saw a great mass of red thrust itself onto the morning sky. By mid-morning, he knew his skin would be baking under the burning sphere.

"Missouri weather," his father said.

George, yawning, moved with little want toward the morning's work of cultivating the hemp rows.

"George, you open that mouth any wider, and it's going to be full of flies."

He laughed at his father's joke, then caught midway between laugh and yawn, began to cough uncontrollably, choked by his action. His father burst out laughing as George tried to regain control of his coughing. Then his father's hand plopped on his shoulder, and all seemed right in his world. The youth of eighteen had worked with his father in the hemp fields since age eight. For as long as he remembered, his father William had been his best friend and teacher. By example, he always inspired George to work hard, and speak proper.

"Son, did you hear cannon fire last night?"

George looked up at his father, trying to remember the previous evening.

"It sounded like it was coming from west of the farm, out near the Little Blue."

"I don't remember hearing any sounds last night, Father." He could see a troubled look on his father's face, the same look his father took on when the hemp quota was short for the week.

"George, I think the war may have finally reached us. It's probably nothing, but stay alert this morning."

"Why? What's going to happen?"

His father's hand left his shoulder. "I don't know, Son. Just stay alert. Now let's get about our work."

George took up his hoe and began breaking the ground around the hemp stalks. The work was back wrenching, and only the strongest of slaves could work the stalks for fourteen hours a day. Over ten years, the harsh labor had transformed George into a lean, muscular six-foot man. The most striking feature of the young slave was his hair. Unlike other slaves at Anderson Farm, George's hair was a mixture of light and dark brown, full, and tightly coiled. His mother often told him, he had the hair of a tribal king.

"This is for Jeff Davis." He smashed the hoe into the rich soil beneath his feet, causing the ground to splatter in all directions. "And this is for Hiram Anderson." He laid the tool to earth once more with a tremendous concussion. Committed to his task, he looked toward his father working the row next to him. He was leaning on his hoe in a statue-like pose with his forehead resting on the back of his hands.

"Father?" George froze. His brain tried to comprehend the event. "Father!"

Then his father collapsed in a heap upon the dark Missouri soil. In a second, George was on his knees next to his father's limp body. He lifted his father's head and stared into his eyes. "Father! What is it? What's wrong?"

"George."

He strained at his father's almost inaudible whisper. "What?" An ashen color had formed on his father's lips.

"Your chance, son."

"I don't understand." George felt the wetness of tears running down his cheeks.

"The army. Run to the army. Be free, son."

His father's mouth began to open and close in a strange rhythm. After an endless time, his muscles surrendered, and his mouth did not open again. Under the hot Missouri sun, his father's eyes rolled slowly toward the sky. He grabbed the lifeless figure and began rocking him back and forth, his father's head pushed into his chest.

George felt a cooling shade cross his back. *Strange*, He thought. There wasn't a cloud in the sky this morning. He felt the sensation of his body being lifted, separating him from his father. He tried to resist, but all of his energy was gone. He felt helpless as his shoulders drooped downward.

Then he was back in the world. He sensed the hands from other slaves trying to comfort him, holding his shoulders, rubbing his arms, moving him away from the field. Several women knelt next to his father's body. They were swaying back and forth, singing aloud an African death chant.

He violently pulled his arms from the Samaritans moving him toward the slave quarters. "My mother!" he cried. "I've got to see my mother." He composed himself by wiping the tears from his face. He would approach his mother as a man. He would bury his father this day; then he would find the Union Army.

He would be free.

Chapter 1

Palmito Ranch, Texas 1865

Free Anderson tasted the strange mixture of dust, acrid smoke, and sweat running from his brow and settling on his lips. A heavy layer of dirty white powder floated head high around his regiment, making all who walked through it take on an eerie, ghost-like complexion. The source of the fume was a barrage of artillery rounds bombarding retreating Union regiments. Free prodded his men, members of the 62nd United States Colored Infantry First Regiment, to quick time their retreat, but to no avail. Each of his soldiers, involved in skirmishes for almost twenty-four hours straight, walked as if mired knee-deep in mud.

The rebels had moved their artillery up in line, and Free heard the shouts and hoorays of the Confederate cavalry carrying across the plain. The land against which the 62nd retreated was no more than a scrub prairie of marsh plants and palmetto trees and offered little in the way of cover. Free was not a stranger to battle, but he could never get accustomed to the sounds and smells of war. The continual bombardment, deafening in its effect, allowed confusion to slip into a man's mind. He had witnessed many a brave soldier, disoriented by wave afterwave of combat, wandering through a battlefield, oblivious of the consequences. The dread of dying wreaked havoc on the human body. It forced the stench of fear out of a man's every pore, leaving the battlefield reeking with the bitter smell of sweat, blood, and piss.

It seemed straightforward that Colonel Barrett was scooped into this fight, and now the exhausted men of his company might pay the price of it. The colonel had ridden to the back of the line only once to order Captain Johansson and forty-six men of the 34th Indiana to break out of formation and scatter as cover for the running retreat. Free knew Captain Johansson to be a first-rate officer and hoped he would fare well against the energized rebel force.

Three miles into the Union retreat, the Confederate bombardments went quiet as the artillery was once again moved forward in their line. Free halted his brigade for a pause and noticed a lone rider from the front moving toward their position. He could tell right away from the rider's low position over the horse's shoulders that the approaching pony carried Union Lieutenant Parks Scott, a volunteer with the 2nd Texas Cavalry and a man Free called friend. He had met Parks when the 62nd first dispatched to Brazos Santiago. The young Cavalry Lieutenant was a first-rate horseman and the sole officer of the 2nd Texas who was still mounted. He held ground when the hornets buzzed about and men around him fled. And when all others shunned the men of the 62nd, Parks Scott would not. He had spent each evening in the colored camps offering to help any man who wanted, to learn to read and write. Free knew the men of the 62nd would ride the river at first call with Parks. He was a man you could tie to.

The paint mustang dug heels into the ground in

front of Free, kicking up rock and powder. The rider, a lean young man of no more than twenty years, leaned over the horse's shoulder and tipped his hat upward, revealing sky-blue eyes.

"Seems you boys are in a might of a pickle back here."

"Oh, it's just a little fuss, Lieutenant." Free moved up close to the paint and stroked the horse's neck. "Chew?" He looked up at his friend.

Parks Scott lifted a leather pouch from around his neck and tossed it into the air. "Your men appear pretty well played out, Sergeant."

Free looked at his lines. He knew from experience a soldier's words might claim the fight, but a man's eyes never disguised fatigue. There was not a doubt in his heart that his men, whipped by exhaustion, needed relief. "Not these men, these men are in apple pie order, sir."

"Well that's good to know because Colonel Barrett has decided to pass the buck back to you and the 62nd while he skedaddles to Boca Chica."

"So that's how it is?" Free cut off a plug of tobacco and pushed it into the back of his jaw.

"Would appear so."

"Well, I appreciate you riding back all this way to let me know."

"I figure it would be best for us to wind up this business so maybe I can go home."

"You plan on staying back here with us?"

"Sergeant," Parks rubbed his pony's neck, "you know this paint is the fastest in South Texas, but he's having a dreadful time keeping up with the 34th. I've never seen men depart a scrape so quick. I figure he deserves a rest back here where the company is more to his liking."

Free let a wide smile come over his face. "Scuttlebutt is Jeff Davis is captured, and his cabinet spread to the wind." Free bit down hard on the tobacco plug, causing the brown juice to flow to the corners of his mouth.

"I've heard that." Parks said.

"And Lee himself has surrendered?" Free asked.

"I've heard that also."

"Not to shirk my responsibility, but doesn't that mean the war is over for these men?" Free spit at a large pad of cactus.

"Not for Colonel Barrett. He was so right and ready to capture Brownsvilie that he failed to consider how the Confederate forces would react. When he broke General Wallace's truce with old Rip Ford, he threw down a challenge to these Texas boys. And now it appears they've got their backs up and aim to make him pay." Parks turned an ear toward the Confederate lines. "I would figure by the commotion behind us and the fact we aren't hearing any report, that Johansson's group is captured or killed."

"That would be a pure tragedy." Free looked back in the same direction as the lieutenant. "What do you figure we need to do to slow down these Graybacks?"

"If it were me, Sergeant, I'd spread my men across this plain, in line and as far apart as possible. Spread out, we might take the artillery out of play. You take one flank, and I'll take the other. I think we all might be game for it."

"Good luck to you, Parks." Free handed the leather pouch back to his friend.

"Try to take care of yourself, Sergeant." Parks

grinned broadly. "I might not have time to come back and save your old hide."

Free watched the lieutenant ride away as he called orders for his men to move out in line across the South Texas plain. For the next three hours, both sides fired on one another with little ambition as to battle. He figured the lateness of the afternoon and exhaustion kept the Confederates from pursuing his troops more vigorously. Near sundown, the incoming artillery diminished, and the 62nd crossed the remaining three miles back to the skiffs.

The exodus scene at the inlet was one of chaos. Many of the Union soldiers from the 34th were jumping on the skiffs, which were used to ferry the soldiers across the Boca Chica inlet, to the safety of Brazos Island, while wounded soldiers lay on blankets near the water. Free watched in horror as the field officer in charge showed little interest in stopping the throng of blue rushing the shoreline. His lack of action allowed the soldiers to run past him undaunted and into the shallow water where the skiffs waited. Free ran to the water's edge, imploring the soldiers to help him move the wounded to the skiffs first. He removed his forage cap and began waving it back and forth. "Hey! Hey!' He screamed toward the frenzied soldiers. "The Rebs have gone! They've all left!"

"Sergeant!" The field officer screamed. "Hobble your lip! We don't need coloreds giving orders to white soldiers and especially not to white officers! Do you understand me?"

Free set a hard gaze on the officer's face. He recognized him from Benton Barracks as Corporal

Jubal Thompson. He was the one officer who continually harassed the soldiers of the 62nd. This mean, hard case of a man enjoyed the suffering of others and took great satisfaction in making the colored soldiers perform fatigue duty long after their normal workday was done. Free bit down on his lip and answered, "Yes sir. Sorry, Corporal Thompson." He knew he had made a serious mistake. For a brief moment, he had allowed himself to forget his color. For a brief moment, he was just a man. The president's orders may have freed him, but it did not make him an equal. He feared a world where he would always be inferior in the eyes of men like Jubal Thompson.

He watched as a broad smirk came over the corporal's face. The look was a familiar one. He had seen it many times as a slave in Missouri. It was the look white men gave the slaves to reinforce that they were not in control of their own lives. Corporal Thompson turned away, back to the chaos, still exerting no control over the situation.

Free took one more look at the scene and moved back to his regiment. He called for roll and took the count. He was relieved to note that not one man of the First Regiment was lost, and only nine men were wounded. He gave his own thanks for this blessing and looked around the group for Parks. He had lost sight of him during the retreat and hoped that the lieutenant made safe passage to the skiffs.

Chapter 2

Tulosa Bluff, Texas 1865

Parks Scott made sure that Free and the men of the 62nd were out of danger and moving without difficulty toward the Boca Chica inlet. He observed that the Texas Cavalry attack had ceased, and the artillery battalion was moving back toward Palmito Ranch. Even after riding over twenty miles this day, he figured he could catch up to them before the soldiers reached the Tulosa Bluff. If he knew Rip Ford, that is where he would bivouac his men. Riding into the Rebel camp was a dangerous affair, but Parks knew that he and the 62nd were expendable in Colonel Barrett's way of thinking. His only hope of avoiding the blame that most certainly would be brought to bear on him and Free was to convince Colonel Ford to vouch for the 62nd.

Parks' father, Wyatt, had ridden with the colonel as a Texas Ranger. The two had chased and fought Indians from Mesquiteville to Fort Cooper during the Canadian River Campaign of '58. He knew that the colonel, no matter what uniform he wore, always carried the respect of other military leaders.

As he raced toward the bluff, he could see the glint of sunlight reflecting off the hill. The point of light gave him a fixed position of the Confederate camp. *Getting careless in your old age colonel*, he thought. He reckoned field glasses were observing him, so in the spirit of showing off, he pushed the pony to top speed, raising a wall of dust behind him.

The paint mustang crested the top of the craggy bluff with little effort and created a small landslide of dirt behind him. Parks heeled the pony and walked him slowly over to a man he had known since he was a small boy. "Colonel Ford." He acknowledged the old family friend.

"That's a fine mount you have there, son."

"He'll do." Parks Scott dismounted and let his reins hit the ground.

"You Union boys took us on quite a run today."

Parks laughed. "Well, Colonel Barrett had his eyes set on seeing the elephant, and I think he took an immediate dislike to the beast." He leaned over and shook the colonel's hand.

"Parks, how are you?"

Parks acknowledged the men around him with a nod of his head and then looked back toward the colonel. "Well, sir."

"So, tell me what brings you so late from battle?"

"I was hoping we might do some horse trading."

"Horse trading, you say. And what is it you have to trade?"

Parks watched as the colonel looked back at his troops. He knew the bargaining was about to begin. No respectable Texan would turn down the chance to one-up a fellow Texan. Bartering was a delicate dance, where a man's words indicated his interest or lack thereof in the deal. To show interest too soon could make a man pay through the nose, just as showing too little interest could head the deal south. Parks knew the colonel was an expert in the art, but he was no shave tail and figured to use that to his advantage. "The war's over, sir."

"And by the looks of today, it appears the Confederacy won."

Parks listened as the colonel's troops guffawed and clapped their hands together. He smiled to himself. "Lee's quit. Jeff Davis is captured, and I hear General Kirby Smith is meeting right now to prepare the surrender of the Trans-Mississippi Confederate troops."

"Son if you're here to surrender, just say so. I'll gladly take your gun and let you keep your pony. We don't need to speak further of the embarrassment."

Parks could barely hold a straight face as the colonel leaned in toward him and spit near his feet. "Begging your pardon, sir, but I think the Texas sun has burnt a fever in your head." He gestured toward the Rebel soldiers. "Surely, you've told these fine men that by next week they'll all be surrendering their arms at Fort Brown." He saw the colonel's expression change ever so slightly. He knew a blink when he saw one and knew he had the advantage.

"These men? Son, next week these men will be drinking whiskey across the river in Old Mexico with their guns still strapped around their waists."

"I hate to disagree sir, but Colonel Barrett has one shot at redemption, and that's to chase down the man who defeated him today."

"Son, if Colonel Barrett wants to ride across the Rio Grande to have a drink with me and the boys, well . . . we would welcome him as an old friend. But as an aside, lieutenant, it was the Mexicans who tipped us off to Colonel Barrett's late night foray into Palmito Ranch. I don't think they'll take too kindly to Union soldiers chasing Texans across the border."

Parks knew this was the time to offer the colonel a way out of the talk with his respectability intact. "Colonel, you know the Union army is going to come looking for you and your men. I'm here to tell you so. I know it goes against being a Texan to surrender to anyone . . . but to have to surrender to the old states . . . I believe that would stick in any respectable Texan's craw." Parks looked around and could see the colonel's men nodding in agreement.

"All I'm hearing, son, is a bunch of words. Union words that barely make any sense. What have you got to offer?"

The trap was set. Parks knew he needed to tread carefully with his proposal. "I was hoping you would give up the 34th Indiana prisoners."

"Now Parks. You are like a son to me, and Lord knows I would do anything for you or your momma, but why on earth would I want to release those prisoners? I most certainly have more leverage with them than without them."

"I reckoned you would want to let these Texas lads go their way." Parks nodded toward the colonel's men. He could see the soldier's intent gazes as they waited for the colonel's response. Parks locked eyes with his old friend.

"So we can't very well scatter if we're carrying a lot of Union deadbeats?"

"That's my take on it, sir." He lifted his eyes ever so slightly toward Rip's face, the proverbial child caught with his hand in the cookie jar. He could see a flush of red on the colonel's neck, but a broad smile told him Rip approved of the grown up facing him.

"You're right, Parks. I figure we have our victory today. And I can find no good reason why we shouldn't be generous with our spoils. This war has taken a toll on this whole country. Maybe it is time to start the healing. I'll see the boys of the 34th get pointed in the right direction."

"Thank you, Colonel. And I offer my word to you if anyone asks; I carry no knowledge as to the whereabouts of the Texas rebels." Parks hesitated and then added, "But sir, there is one more thing."

"Parks, you would try a gospel sharp's patience. What else?"

"Colonel, given the opportunity, I would appreciate your making it known that the 62nd negotiated the prisoner's release. It's important to me."

"Parks, I'll give it some thought. Take care of yourself. Your daddy would be proud to see what a man you've become."

Parks swung up on his pony and looked down at the colonel. "That means more to me than anything that happened out here today, sir."

"Come see me when you muster out, Parks. I can always use a good man."

"I'll do that. But right now, I need to get back to Brazos Santiago. My gut tells me there is going to be blame dealt on the rout today. And there's a group of soldiers back there that will need my help once the big bugs start talking."

The colonel nodded his understanding and slapped the mustang's flank. "Adios, son."

"Adios, Colonel Ford."

Chapter 3

Outside of Fort Brown, Texas 1865

F ree sat outside of his tent chewing tobacco and staring with great concentration at the dirt beneath his feet. Fort Brown was awash with activity this June day. General Slaughter and Colonel Ford had ridden into camp before noon. News traveled fast through the post, and within minutes of the two Confederate officers arrival, word traveled down tent row that General Slaughter was there to negotiate their personal surrender. At the same time in Galveston, General Kirby Smith had arrived to sign the terms of surrender of the remaining Confederate armies. But other news was also working its way through camp, a rumor as to the reason for Colonel Ford's presence in the Fort. Some were saying he had been asked to provide his account of the Palmito Ranch battle to a military board. If that were true, the higher ups would be deflecting blame downhill in quick order. Someone would have to take the blame for the battlefield retreat and the loss of over a hundred Union soldiers at what now appeared to be the last battle of the great war. And Free had a good idea where that cascading blame would land.

Parks had spent thirty minutes with Colonel Ford upon his arrival, and Free had watched both men in a long discussion. After the talk had quit, Colonel Ford had shaken hands with Parks and walked up the stairs to the adjutant-general's quarters.

Free noted that Parks seemed deep in his thoughts as he moved back toward tent row. For the first day in over a month, the 62nd had time off to relax. There were neither drills nor fatigue duty this day. Free had watched the white officers inside the Fort move from group to group talking in hushed tones. He did not see good things coming from these conversations for either himself or his men. This day of rest laid more weight to his shoulders than a whole day on the battlefield.

"Those officers in the Fort seem all balled up."

"Well they sure have me spooked." Free pulled a commissary crate from behind his tent flap and motioned for Parks to sit. "I have never seen such activity running through a camp after the fighting is quit."

He watched as his friend took a seat on the crate and pulled his cap off his head. "There are more than a few officers inside that fort worried they are about to be nailed to the counter."

"We both know what happened on that scrub prairie, Parks, but what gets written as record will be scribed by higher up than a sergeant or a lieutenant rank. And it doesn't have to be the truth."

"What's poking you in the gut, Free?"

Free turned from Parks and directed his gaze down tent row. The men of the 62nd were busy this morning. Some cleaned dishes in a kettle, while others stacked wood. All were smiling or laughing during their chores. "I guess I'm worried that everything my men set out to prove is going to be tossed aside with little thought. We all joined to fight and to give our lives if needed. This was necessary to show we deserved our freedoms. But, it appears our freedom begins and ends on the battlefield. These are all good men, Parks. I'll bet none of those soldiers in the fort knows that the men of the 62nd give a little bit of their pay each month in the hope that, someday, their money will be enough to build a school. A place where all freedmen can learn to read, and write, and be educated. So, yes, I'm worried. Worried that after today, the 62nd will be labeled as men filled with laziness. Cowards, who sidestepped their duties. And if that is the day's outcome, many freedmen will be lying in the bone orchard with nothing to show for their sacrifice. These men deserve the better of things."

He took a long look at Parks' face and could see by the furrowed brow that the lieutenant had something on his mind. Waiting in anticipation, he watched as his friend rubbed the top of his head and replaced his cap.

"Free, I think you can rest easy about your men shouldering the blame for Palmito Ranch. When Colonel Barrett hears what Colonel Ford intends to say to the adjutant-general tribunal, I believe he will write his report giving gracious comments to all involved. He is going to be especially eloquent in his reciting of the 62nd First Regiment's actions."

Free pursed his lips tight. "Why would he do that?"

"He is going to do that because Colonel Ford will have spoken to him in quiet prior to the hearing as commanding officer to commanding officer. The colonel will tell him that the release of forty-six men of the 34th Indiana was precipitated by negotiations from a colored sergeant of the 62nd. He will also inform the colonel that he had never seen an army depart a battle as fast as Barrett's troops did that day."

"So who gets the blame for the loss of over one hundred men? If not the 62nd, who?

"That could be your problem; I pray the good that happens today does not cause unjust problems for you down the road."

Free was puzzled. "What is it? What problems?"

"Jubal Thompson, the field officer in charge at the Boca Chica crossing, is going to get it in the neck. You were the only one who confronted him, and he is going to remember that. He is going to remember that for a long time after he musters out. You know the man, Free; he is not going to accept an ex-slave holding control over his lack of duty. But that is the only option Colonel Ford felt Colonel Barrett would accept. Someone lower than the colonel has to take the blame."

Free took a moment to chew on Park's comments. He understood exactly what Parks was telling him. "It's not like he isn't guilty. Lots of men died that night. Men who should be alive today." Free studied the lieutenant's face. "I believe I can live with that, no matter what comes my way."

"Just be careful. He's the sort to carry a grudge down a long road."

Chapter 4

Anderson Farm, Missouri 1866

Free had been walking across the Missouri landscape for several days. It was as pretty an April day as he could ever remember. The spring rains must have been plentiful, for the green lushness of the land enveloped the countryside.

In March, his regiment mustered out honorably at Benton Barracks. After his military release, he was determined to get back home, even if it meant walking across Missouri. He needed to find his mother. She deserved to know her son was alive and well.

On the sixth day at around noon, Free took in the view of Anderson Farm from a small rise on the road from Independence. Almost two years had passed since he left the farm in a run through the hemp fields away from his slavery. Smoke rose from the main house chimney, but the farm itself was strangely quiet. He could not see any movement in the fields or hear the normal noise of a working farm. He crossed over the road through what should have been a field of emerging hemp stalks. Instead, the ground was hard and unturned. A feeling of unease came over him, and he began to quicken his pace, moving straight for the house.

The Anderson house yard, usually alive with peafowl, chickens, and guinea hens, was void of any animal. Free stopped and looked tentatively at the back porch door. Two years ago, he would have been beaten for daring to venture onto this part of the farm without Hiram's permission. Now, even as a freedman, he hesitated, waiting for that permission to be granted.

"George Washington?"

Free turned, half startled by the sound of his slave name.

"Is that you, George?"

He instantly recognized the woman standing to his left. There could be no mistaking the oversized apron and the way she held her head, always upright and proud. "Mother."

The gray-haired woman brought the apron's edge to her eyes. "It is you, George. We thought we'd never see you again." She held her arms out toward her son.

Free moved to her, bending down to hold her tightly. "I wrote to you. I still have the letter in my pocket. I just didn't have anybody to deliver it to you."

Martha Anderson pushed back from her son. "Let me look at you. You've grown so straight and tall. Your father would be so proud of you." She moved back in close and held her firstborn as tears flowed down her cheeks.

"Mother, where is everyone? Why is it so quiet here? What—."

His mother pushed a finger to his mouth. "You've come a long way." She gleamed proudly at Free and wiped her eyes. "We'll talk after you get some food inside of you." She abruptly turned and walked toward the back door.

Free breathed deep, letting his nose carry the smells of childhood throughout his body. The aroma of fried hog back and eggs drifted from the cook stove and soon found hold in every crevice of the Anderson farmhouse. He held his coffee cup in both hands, inhaling the smell of chicory wisping upwards.

His mother wrapped her apron around the skillet handle and moved it from the stovetop. Near the back door, she reached into a small burlap sack and removed a scoop of river sand used to clean the cooking pans. She poured the sand into the skillet until the bottom was coated and then set the pan on the floor. Turning back to Free she sat near him at the table.

"Mother, what is going on here? Where is everyone?"

She held her son's hand and patted it gently. "So much has changed in so short a period of time, George. Men came later in the spring after you ran. They told Mr. Hiram that he was holding runaway slaves, and they were taking them back to their rightful owner."

Free leaned in close to his mother. "What men? Who were they?"

"I don't know, son. They were white men in soldier clothes. Mr. Hiram told the man that these boys were the property of his farm, and they belonged to him. The white man doing all the talking got off his horse and hit Mr. Hiram. He hit him again and again. Soon Mr. Hiram didn't get up anymore. Miss Mary ran out, and the man hit her too."

"What about the others? Joshua and Solomon and their families?" Free gripped his mother's hand firmly. "Where are they, Mother?"

"They took them, George. They took them away in ropes. It's been almost two years now."

"But what about you? Did they try to take you too?"

"George, who would want a sixty-eight-year-old slave woman? They only took what would bring them money."

Free leaned back in his chair and pushed both hands to his face. "So who is running the farm? Who does the planting? How are you surviving?"

Martha looked squarely into her son's eyes. "I am running the farm, George. With Mr. Hiram dead, and the others all gone, there was nobody left to work. And Miss Mary hasn't been out of bed in these two years. Ever since that day. I couldn't leave her. I couldn't let her die."

Free smiled at his mother and remembered the strength she always showed in the hardest of times. "I know you couldn't. But how are you paying for things?"

"I don't know how to explain it, George. I just am. I just do it."

"Mother, I am so proud of you, and I am so proud to see you."

Martha smiled briefly before her face became solemn. "George, there's more. Some other white men came through here in early March. These were hard-looking white men. They asked about an ex-slave. Said his name was Free Anderson. I told them we didn't know anybody here by that name. That man said if I was lying, he would come back and beat me with a strap."

Free could feel a rush of goose bumps rise on his forearms. Only Union soldiers would know of Free Anderson. "What did these white men look like, Mother?"

"They looked like Union soldiers. Except they

only wore the soldier coats. They were talking about you, weren't they George? You're Free Anderson, aren't you?"

"Mother, I'm going to take you away from here tomorrow. It's too dangerous for a woman to be alone in this place."

"George Washington Anderson! I am not going anywhere. I have Miss Mary upstairs sick and all. I will not leave."

Free knew his mother's will and knew it was impossible to try to move her. "Okay, Mother. You're right. I'll stay awhile to get the farm back into working shape for you and Miss Mary."

"George, why did you change your name?"

Free thought back to that day on the road to Independence and suddenly began laughing uncontrollably. His mother was so taken in by the belly laugh that she began to laugh along with her son.

After several minutes, Free fought to control his laughter and finally composed himself enough that he could recount his story. "When I left the afternoon that father died, I ran for several miles without stopping. At the east end of the Little Blue River, I ran headlong into a group of Union soldiers. They ordered me over to their commander, a colonel by the name of Moonlight. I must tell you, he was some presence to a runaway slave. Anyway, Colonel Moonlight tells me I'm free. And then wants to know my name. I was so overwhelmed; all I could say was "Free." So he says to me, "Well, Free, let's get on to Independence." Free slapped the table with his hand and began to belly laugh once more.

"Free." His mother joined in, "I like it."

* * *

The next morning, Free awoke once more to the smell of fried meat in the kitchen. He looked around the room he was in and realized for the first time in his life he was sleeping inside a white man's house. He rose up and took in the room's setting. The bed was soft and comfortable. There were several pieces of furniture in the room and a gold framed mirror on the wall. This was a house his mother deserved to live in. She had toiled all her life, and he reckoned a reward was due her. He made a promise that morning. He would make her a home just like Anderson Farm before she died.

Chapter 5

Anderson Farm, Missouri 1867

F ree cinched the Spanish saddle around Hiram Anderson's horse. The animal was tall,
standing almost seventeen hands. He could
still remember Hiram walking the horse in the
hemp fields and observing each day's work. The
horse always seemed stately to Free. It was odd, he
thought, that he would now be riding the animal.

He turned to his mother, standing with him in
the barn and handed her a small leather sack with
Union coins inside. "Mother, please make sure
Miss Mary gets the money for Mr. Hiram's horse.
Tell her I'll take care of him just as Mr. Hiram al-
ways did."

Martha nodded her head in acknowledgement
of her son's instructions.

"You keep the rest of the money. I don't know
what awaits me out there, but I promise just as
soon as I can get back, I will come for you."

"Don't you worry, George. Me and Miss Mary
will get along just fine here. You do what you need
to do."

Free took his mother into his arms and held her
close. He could not believe eight months had
passed since he arrived back at the farm. "I'll be
back for you."

Martha pushed back slightly, taking a deep gaze
at her son. "I know you will, George. I'll be here
waiting for your return."

Free put a boot up in the stirrup and with little effort swung up on the horse.

"Where will you go, son?"

"Texas."

Martha walked out of the open barn, alongside her son.

"Good-bye, Mother. Take good care of yourself. I aim to make you proud."

He gently took spurs to the horse, leaving his mother behind him. Inside, he felt a strong urge to look back, to say something more. But he decided the better of it. There was no more to be said. The sound of the horse's shoes on the hard ground made an unforgettable sound in his ears. From his back, a light breeze brushed against his shirt. It had the feel of his mother's touch, gently pushing him away from the farm and toward Texas.

Chapter 6

Fort Riley, Kansas, 1867

Slack, Horse." Parks Scott eased his mustang to a slow trot as he entered the lower parade ground at Fort Riley, Kansas. He held a string of five paint mustangs behind him. It was a beautiful Sunday morning at the fort, and many of the soldiers sat outside of their barracks enjoying the newly arrived spring.

Shortly after mustering out of the army in the spring of 1867, Parks had received a letter from Colonel Ford containing information that a great opportunity was about to present itself. According to the colonel, the United States Army was preparing to form a new cavalry unit responsible for controlling the Indians across the southern plains. And the cavalry would need mounts. As the colonel put it, *the kind of horses you know how to capture and train.*

The colonel's letter had put into motion a plan that Parks hoped would flourish after his trip to Fort Riley today.

The roar of laughter snapped Parks' attention back to the post. He listened to the insults issuing from the porch of the 7th Cavalry barracks as he rode by. No matter what military post he rode through, the commonplace jeers and insults were always similar in their rancor.

"Look at the little ponies!"

"Hey cowboy, your horse seems to be between hay and grass!"

The six mustangs stood only fourteen hands high, a foot shorter than the standard cavalry horse on the post. His personal mustang, Horse, stood only fifty-five inches at the withers.

Horse, a paint, was marked as the Comanche preferred with a splotch of color wrapping over his shoulder and around his chest. Parks leaned close in to Horse's ear and whispered, "We'll see who laughs in a bit." The horse seemed to understand, lifted his head high, and began a proud trot in front of the 7th.

Parks stopped his horse at the end of the parade grounds near the flagpole. A contingent of military personnel waited nearby, three figures standing at the front of the group.

"Lieutenant Scott?"

"Not anymore." He swung down from Horse and took a minute to settle his back. He had ridden, this day alone, for almost sixty miles. Twisting his neck back and forth, he looked at the three men standing before him. "Sorry, I'm a might stiff." Two of the men cut a fine figure. Both had long flowing hair that laid shoulder length. The one with golden yellow hair was wearing a military uniform. The other had brownish hair and was dressed in buckskin.

"Mr. Scott, I am General Hancock." The oldest of the three, a most distinguished looking gentleman spoke to Parks.

Parks sized up the officer in front of him and acknowledged his rank. "My pleasure, General. I have heard only the best words about you and your command."

"That is very kind of you, sir." The general pointed to the officer standing to his immediate right, the man with the long golden hair. "This is Lieutenant Colonel Custer. He is the officer responsible for organizing and establishing the cavalry here at the fort."

"Lieutenant Colonel Custer, it is my pleasure."

Custer nodded to Parks and walked toward the pony string.

The third man, who wore a wide brimmed scout's hat, did not wait for introductions and immediately struck his hand towards Parks. "These are some interesting animals you brought with you, Mr. Scott. Allow me to introduce myself; I am James Butler Hickok, a military scout for the general."

Parks knew of this man, for he was one of only a few men alive whose largeness of character and deed were well documented throughout the West.

"Mr. Hickok, your reputation precedes you. It is an honor to meet you in person."

The man, simply known as Wild Bill, smiled graciously. "Pardon my judgment. But do you seriously believe these animals to be superior to our cavalry mounted steeds?"

Before Parks could answer, Lieutenant Colonel Custer spoke in a stern authoritative tone. "I hope I am not speaking out of turn General, but these animals do not look like horses our cavalry would be so inclined to ride."

Parks could see genuine displeasure issuing from General Hancock's face.

"Please excuse the lieutenant colonel's brusqueness. He is of a background where it is better to speak one's mind than to hold a courteousy." The general spoke in an apologetic tone.

"No harm to me or my animal's sir. I came per your request, as a favor of a friend."

"Colonel Ford?"

"Yes sir. I owe the colonel much, and I felt obligated to follow this one." Parks knew that the Indian mustang could only be verified as a superior horse if allowed to run against an American horse. "I am at your disposal, General. I was made aware that you might want to put these horses to the test."

"I think that is the fair value of proceeding." General Hancock responded. "But first, some food for you and your animals is in order. We'll let them rest today and begin right away tomorrow with the test."

Lieutenant Colonel Custer was rubbing his hand down Horse's front shoulder. "If these animals are as hardy as Mr. Scott claims, why would they need a rest?" He turned and looked Parks square in the eye.

Parks knew he was being trifled with. And he knew Custer was coppering his bet by the challenge. "Whatever would be best for you, sir. My horses will run or rest. It matters not either way." Parks tried to remain calm, but he could feel the hairs on the back of his neck rise. He hoped no one else noticed his uncomfortable position.

"It seems, General, lunch would be in order and afterwards a race or two," Wild Bill offered.

General Hancock shook his head in acknowledgment of the military scout's compromise. "Well, if we are all in agreement, let us move for nourishment."

The general had arranged for lunch to be taken in his quarters. The commanding officer's quarters were constructed with a foyer that separated the general's bedroom and study on one side from a small dining room and kitchen on the other.

The smell of pork roast, potatoes, and hot coffee drifted through the room, causing Parks' stomach to growl like a hungry beast. He placed a hand over his stomach and smiled to the group. "Sorry, as you can hear, my stomach is causing a fuss over the smell of cooked food."

The others grinned in understanding.

"Don't fret, Parks." The general responded. "We've all returned from the field with similar results from the smell of a home cooked meal." He pointed to the served table. "Please, everyone, be seated."

The men sat at the meal for the better part of an hour filling themselves with both food and conversation.

Lieutenant Colonel Custer was the first to push back from the table. He leaned back in his chair, removing a bag of tobacco from his shirt pocket. "So tell us, Mr. Scott, what kind of test do you think fairly judges your animals?"

Parks thought on the question while he took one more drink of coffee. "It really does not matter, Lieutenant Colonel Custer. My horses are of mettle to perform at one thousand yards or one thousand miles. I think the bigger question might be what test do you want your army horses to excel at?"

Wild Bill looked at both men and put his napkin to the table. "Tell us of your test, Parks. How is it run?"

"Well sir, we usually take one mustang off the string, and he will compete against any or all of your army horses."

Parks could see the bewilderment in the military men's eyes.

"Are you telling us you will run only one of your horses against however many animals we want to test?"

"Yes, General. I've found that appears the best way to get the army's attention. In previous tests, I don't think I've been a disappointment yet."

The general slapped his knee in glee. "By God. I am anxious to watch this exhibition. Lieutenant Colonel, have your men pick out the three best horses we have on post." He looked at Parks and opened the lid to a small rectangular box that sat in the middle of the table. "Cigar?"

Parks waved his hand in front of his chest. "No thank you, sir. I've never been able to master that skill."

"Well here's what I choose Parks. We will run a test at one thousand yards, one test at two thousand yards and the final test at three thousand yards. What do you say to that?"

"I think that should be a good test, sir."

Lieutenant Colonel Custer stood from the table. "If you gentlemen will excuse me, I will arrange the test field and get the army animals ready." He made a military about face and exited the dining area.

Wild Bill removed a cigar from the general's box. "General, the Lieutenant Colonel seems to be wound very tight."

"It's his style. Make no mistake; he is a very serious officer with much ambition. I would bet a box of those cigars he rides the last test."

Parks looked at his fellow diners. "Well, that is probably how it should be."

General Hancock nodded in agreement. "Shall we?" He motioned both men toward the door.

Chapter 7

Fort Riley, Kansas 1867

The post was buzzing with activity. Most days for the soldiers on the frontier involved plenty of manual labor and a wagonload of boredom. With word trickling through the fort that a horse race was set for the afternoon, everyone had eagerly joined in the preparations.

Three men stepped out of the officers' quarters into a bright spring day. General Hancock stopped at the foot of the stairs and took a match to his cigar. "So tell me Parks, how do the savages train their horses to be as strong as you indicate?"

"Actually, General, the horses come born with a hundred years of a strong survival instinct. Their ancestors ran wild across the Texas plains. Nature took the weakest of them, and those that survived were the ultimate war mount. My horses can live off a pasture of rocks and still run a hundred miles a day with little effort."

Wild Bill drew deep on his cigar, exhaling a long fume of smoke towards the April sky. "General, I hope you would not object to a wager put to our horseman."

"As long as your intentions are for relief from the boredom associated with this post, I could not see any harm."

"Would you be willing to help break the boredom of my day, Parks?"

Parks noticed a gleam in the scout's eye. "Begging your pardon, Mr. Hickok, but I would find myself contemptible for purposely taking a man's hard-earned money."

Wild Bill took pause and laughed with great force. "Please, sir, do not worry on my account; it is rare that any of my money would be hard earned."

Parks walked over to his string and untied a brown-flecked animal he called Little Star. The horse's eyes were clear and showed a sparkle as Parks held his reins. Parks knew this excitement meant he was ready to run. He slipped a six-braided hackamore over Little Star's nose and brought the reins back to his neck. Like the Indians, he hand-braided his hackamores with a combination of buffalo hide and horsehair. Little Star was particularly impatient with the bit, and Parks respected his temperament never allowing iron in the mustang's mouth. He patted the animal's forehead and rubbed a wet rag down his forelegs and side. "Little Star," he whispered almost inaudibly in the horse's ear. "Let's go for a run."

Lieutenant Colonel Custer had three fine-looking army horses awaiting him at the starting line. The horses were all a rich brown color and showed the obvious signs of excellent grooming. All three stood at least seventeen hands high or a little over five and one half feet at the withers. Like most army mounts, the animals were tall with long necks.

The difference in the competing animals was even more pronounced as they stood side by side. Little Star was short and compact with a thick neck. The army horse towered over the Indian pony, and, judging by appearance, it seemed the more qualified animal.

Lieutenant Colonel Custer walked to the front of both steeds and pressed his hands against each animal's nose. "Mr. Scott, the first test will run for one thousand yards." The lieutenant colonel pointed down the quickly prepared track to a man holding the 7th Cavalry's colors. The race lane was flat, and littered with small rocks. It sloped so the return was slightly uphill. "At the colors, you will need to turn and come back to this line. It is approximately five hundred yards to that point. When the sergeant fires his pistol, you may proceed."

Parks listened to the instructions while taking a quick inventory of the starter and the lane of soldiers who lined either side of the track. He turned back to the starting line and looked over at his competition. In the spirit of fair play, he nodded to the soldier sitting on the cavalry mount next to him. "Good luck to you." With a pull of the rein, he moved Little Star several feet away from the army horse. "I am ready whenever it is convenient, Lieutenant Colonel Custer."

He watched in anticipation as the lieutenant colonel spoke to his sergeant. "At your pleasure, sergeant."

The gun seemed to discharge without a moment's hesitation. The army horse rose slightly and raced from the line. Little Star had no wasted motion, neither rearing nor raising his head. He moved in complete timing with the gunfire. The mustang threw his head into the wind and never lifted it as he hit the halfway mark with a thirty-yard lead over the cavalry steed. In a matter of seconds, he had completed his turn and was back at the line exerting little effort.

"Bejesus!" Wild Bill swung his hat in a wide arc

around his head. "If that don't take the rag off the bush!"

The entire lane of soldiers was strangely silent, as the army horse finished up some forty yards behind Little Star.

"It would seem that you have made good on your pronouncement of this horse's fitness." Parks listened to the general's comments and looked over to Custer. He could see that the lieutenant colonel was boiling inside. Although his face remained calm, he could not hide the red flush spreading across his forehead. Parks nodded to the general acknowledging his thanks.

"We'll see after he tests the next two mounts," Lieutenant Colonel Custer offered.

Little Star, flush with energy, had every hair on his mane standing at attention. The second army horse, another magnificent-looking animal was led to the line. Little Star took a glance at the animal and moved his head back and forth as if to personally challenge the steed. "Slack," Parks spoke in a quiet tone to the horse. As the sergeant's Colt revolver roared once more, Little Star exploded down the track. The army mount stayed close, but the extended track proved hard on the animal. At the turn, Little Star dipped his shoulder, dug his heels in tight, and dropped his back end. The result was a very tight circle around the 7th's colors, and a plume of dust sprayed toward the private holding the standard.

Parks could feel the mustang's power beneath him. A ripple of flexing muscles moved with the mustang's every step. He saw the horse turn his head back slightly, as if he wanted the other horse to run with him. Given the hesitation by Little Star,

the army steed roared back head-to-head with
Parks. Parks could see the cavalry soldier grin in
anticipation of his victory. "Com'on Little Star,"
Parks whispered. "This is not a good time to play."
He watched as the pony glanced at the army horse,
nodding his head up and down at the animal. As if
on cue, Little Star gave a whinny, looked up the
track, and with a burst of speed shot ahead, finishing twenty-five yards in front of the army steed.

Parks turned Little Star back around toward the
starting line. He kept his desire to grin in check as
he did not want to insult the army riders. But inside, he could feel the warmth of victory spreading
through his body. He imagined that Lieutenant
Colonel Custer was as hot as a pepper right about
now.

Parks looked on as the lieutenant colonel mounted
his horse, a muscular dark brown animal called
Dandy. The horse walked proudly to the starting
line. Parks could immediately sense that this horse
was a proud beast with a high spirit of competition.

"Mr. Scott, I trust now you will receive an ade-
quate test for your pony."

Parks could see the visible anger on his oppo-
nent. "A fine animal you sit on, sir," he offered as
respect to the lieutenant colonel.

Before Parks could set, he noticed Lieutenant
Colonel Custer motion his right arm toward the
sergeant and heard the gun discharge. The lieutenant colonel had begun forward with Dandy a
split second before the gun, leaving Parks com-
menting to the now-empty space where Dandy
had stood seconds before.

Little Star did not need encouragement or permission from Parks to begin. He followed the taller horse off the line, his hooves thundering down the track. Parks regained his composure and lay low over Little Star's neck, urging his steed on. Custer reached the standard seconds before Parks and completed a tight turn. Little Star reached the colors and, upon finishing his turn, exploded with a burst of speed that propelled him down the track. Custer's lead now narrowed. Parks could see the lieutenant colonel flash his whip, beating his horse toward the finish. From Little Star's nose, he watched great puffs of steam blow, superheated from his exertion. With a slight nudge of his spurs, Parks whispered into the mustang's left ear. "It's time to go, Little Star." Instantly, he felt all tension from beneath the saddle fade and watched the pony extend his front legs into graceful but powerful strides. Running as a mustang in the wild, Little Star blared past Dandy, finishing a full length ahead. As Custer crossed the line behind Parks, Dandy pulled up hard with a noticeable limp.

Parks looked back and saw the men of the 7th running to the lieutenant colonel, grabbing Dandy's bridle and helping the steed come to a stop. Lieutenant Colonel Custer rolled off Dandy and cursed loudly.

Parks dismounted and rubbed Little Star's ears. "Good, Little Star. Good." Parks dropped the reins, and Little Star walked, head down, back to the string.

"A truly amazing display of the Indian pony, Parks. I was skeptical, but I will not argue with what I witnessed here today."

"Thank you, General Hancock."

"Let's leave the lieutenant colonel to his own and move back to my quarters for a talk."

"Yes sir." Parks looked back over his shoulder to see if he could determine the depth of Dandy's leg injury.

Inside the general's quarters, Parks sat in a cowhide high-back chair. The general walked over to a small table where a glass canister containing his favorite Scotch sat. He held the bottle toward Parks. "Drink?"

"No thank you, sir."

"My God, Parks! I am impressed. Those ponies of yours travel sixty miles in eight hours, take a two-hour rest, and beat the best we have to offer handily. No wonder we can't keep up with the savages." He took a long drink of his Scotch. "It troubles me to say so, but I cannot and will not purchase any of those animals, son."

Parks looked at the general confused.

"As much as I agree, those animals are significantly better mounts than what the 7th currently rides, I am still of the belief that this Indian engagement will be won by showing the cavalry's might. I find it hard to believe we will show our might riding into battle on small ponies, no matter their endurance."

"General, you are the one judged by your decisions. I learned many years ago not to declare opinions as to another man's thinking."

"Thank you, Parks. You are as Colonel Ford said I would find you."

"I appreciate your compliment, General." Parks rose from his seat and walked over to shake the general's hand. "I will ask your leave now. I think it's time to get back to Texas."

The General tipped his glass toward Parks. "Ride safe."

As he walked across the lower parade ground toward his string, Parks noticed Wild Bill admiring his horses.

"So, Parks, how many will the general take?" The army scout rubbed Little Star's ear gently.

"None at the present. The general feels these ponies do not fairly represent the U.S. Cavalry's might."

The army scout looked bewildered. "Well, I am in disagreement but not surprised. I learned a long time ago to judge neither man nor beast as to their appearance. Things do not survive in the frontier because of their size. But, each man is entitled to an opinion as to the solution for the Indian problem. What do you think Parks?"

"I find a man has little fuss in his life if he sticks to his own business."

"You may be wise beyond your years. Where to now?"

"Back to Texas. But I would ask a favor."

"I think I could give you that. What do you need me to do?"

"I would ask that you present Lieutenant Colonel Custer with a gift as the opportunity would present itself. It appeared his mount may be crippled." Parks cut loose the taller of his ponies, a multi-colored horse with a dark splay on his forehead. He handed the rein to Wild Bill. "His name is Morning Sun. Please ask Lieutenant Colonel Custer to accept him with my best wishes."

"That I will do, my friend, but do you really think this gift is going to soothe the lieutenant colonel's anger?"

Parks knew Wild Bill was correct. He had no choice but to defeat the cavalry mounts, but he might have created a bigger problem with selling future ponies to the calvary by embarrassing the lieutenant colonel. He was sure of one thing; he had created an enemy today. An enemy with the United States Cavalry square at his back.

Chapter 8

Clear Fork Country, Texas 1868

Free moved the remuda herd cautiously through a small ravine near the Clear Fork of the Brazos. He looked up the trail and could see that Mr. Goodnight had skirted the main herd to catch up with the chuck wagon. The Clear Fork was at its widest here, and the clean water flowed quickly over a bed of gravel and small rocks.

"Free!"

He could see Goodnight signaling for him to move the remuda herd up to the evening campsite.

Free whistled loudly and directed the herd up the opposite side of the ravine and onto a wide grassy area that sloped down toward the river. The horses, heads down, eagerly pulled up the fresh slips of spring grasses.

"Yes sir, Mr. Goodnight?"

The slender veteran of the trail walked up to his wrangler. "Coyo tells me there should be buffalo just beyond the next rise. He says they run this area every May for the clover. You think the men would enjoy a bison steak this evening?"

"Oh yes sir, Mr. Goodnight." Free could feel the saliva take hold in his mouth at the mention of steak.

"Well, take my Henry and see what you can find." Goodnight handed the pristine buffalo gun up to Free's out-stretched hand. "I'll watch the remuda. You just be careful and make sure you stay downwind from us. I don't need any cattle running this evening."

"Yes sir." Free positioned the heavy rifle across his saddle.

"And, Free, that barrel will get hot as a skillet the more shots you take, so my advice to you is make your kill with one shot."

Free grinned at the trail boss. "I understand, Mr. Goodnight. I won't be back with any blisters."

Goodnight looked back to the east. "I think Bose is about an hour back the trail, so you best hurry. You need only cut out the back-strap and the hindquarters. The coyotes might stay quiet tonight if we share a little of our bounty with them."

Free nodded his head and put his spurs gently to Hiram Anderson's horse, now known as "Comida." One of the Mexican drovers, Georges, took to calling the animal by this handle as it took every opportunity presented to eat. The rest of the group, even Mr. Goodnight, who was usually business only, had laughed and taken to calling the horse by its new Mexican name. Free joined in the good-natured fun, as it seemed to make his acceptance in the group go easier.

"Let's go, Comida." He pushed the horse west. Nearly a mile or so from the chuck wagon, Free came upon a site that would silence even the most grizzled buffalo hunter. Set in front of him in a small valley were thousands and thousands of buffalo. The whole of the valley was dark with the curly-haired beasts. He pushed up in the stirrups to stretch his back and saw a young bull forty or so yards downhill from him. Free quieted Comida and stepped down from the saddle. He pulled down on the horse's reins and at the same time pushed on his hindquarters. Comida slowly bent his front legs and set his belly on the hard ground. Free moved toward the horse's middle and lay the Henry over the saddle, holding the reins tight in his left hand. "Easy, Comida." He whispered to the horse as he drew his sight on the unknowing bull. With a squeeze of the trigger, the great beast went down to his knees. Comida, startled at the shot, kept his voice, but took to his feet instantly. At the same time, Free put a boot in the stirrup and was on the horse. No member of the great herd moved or seemed startled as he rode down the hill to his kill.

His shot had been true, hitting the buffalo behind the left shoulder. Free stepped down from Comida and removed a skinner's knife from his boot. He knelt near the buffalo and started a straight cut down each side of the animal's backbone. He made cuts above the ribs and moved the knife upward until he could cut away large chunks of meat two feet long by six inches wide. As he prepared to lay the meat hide side down on the back of his saddle, he caught movement out of the corner of his eye. Silhouettes, highlighted against the western sky, moved slowly in column from north to south. He stayed in a crouched position behind Comida and counted six figures moving across the horizon on the far side of the valley. "Easy, Comida," he whispered to the animal.

The figures didn't show interest in the buffalo or the rifle shot. But Mr. Goodnight had warned him before, that riders moving around a drive herd almost always meant no good for the cowboys. He figured he best get back to camp and warn the trail boss. Working feverishly, he took his knife to the animals' hindquarters and cut out each roast. He reckoned each weighed ten pounds. He loaded all the meat into a burlap sack and hung it over his saddle horn. In a matter of minutes, he was heading back toward the chuck wagon with a strange sense of dread stirring around in his head.

Free rode Comida hard into camp. A lather of foam dotted the horse's bit. He heeled the animal so strongly that Comida's hindquarters nearly touched the ground, kicking a splay of dust into the air.

"Whoa!" Coyo yelled at the horse and rider. "What's gotten into you, Free?"

Free let up on the reins, allowing Comida to right himself. "Where's Mr. Goodnight?" he asked urgently. He tossed the burlap sack of meat to the Indian cook.

"Trouble?" Coyo asked as he caught the sack.

"Could be. I don't know." He turned Comida's head to his right and located the trail boss. He was moving in a hurried pace up from the banks of the Brazos.

"Trouble out there?" Goodnight called out.

Free pushed his hat back and dismounted Comida. He recognized the noticeable concern in Goodnight's voice. "There are riders out there, sir. Six at least, maybe more."

"Damn!" Goodnight slapped his hat across his thigh. "Could you tell if they were Indians or others?" he asked, his head turned to the east.

Free reckoned Goodnight's thoughts were on the herd some half mile back on the trail.

"I don't mind the savages; they usually only

want some beeves. It's the other that always concerns me."

"I couldn't tell, sir. I could only see their silhouettes against the sun." Free looked back from where he rode and pointed slightly south of the clover field. "They were coming around our south flank, or that's what it looked like to me."

"Coyo, you better get the ammo box out of the wagon. Much as I hate having guns around the herd, we're not left with any other option tonight."

Free knew from his few conversations with the drovers, that Goodnight's biggest fear was not Indians, rustlers or lightning, but the chance that a young drover might accidentally discharge a pistol around a thousand head of cattle. "You need for me to ride back to get Bose?"

"We'll both go," Goodnight answered. "Keep that Henry with you for now."

Free nodded in understanding.

"Coyo, hurry up with that ammo box, and, Free, you best fill your pockets with shells."

Ammo in hand, Free and Goodnight set spurs to their mounts, leaving camp with intent purpose. They rode abreast at a hard gallop, heading for the front line of the drive herd. A half mile out of camp, Free saw the string of longhorns spread over a mile or more of landscape. At the sight of the herd, he gently pulled Comida's reins right, making sure the horse skirted the herd's flank in as wide an arc as possible. He could feel Goodnight in close tandem.

The two men brought their steeds to a halt at a small cluster of cottonwoods.

"Free, get Bose and Shorty's attention. Call 'em up to join us," Goodnight instructed.

Free stood high in his saddle and began gesturing a series of signals toward the front line drovers. Bose Ikard, also an ex-slave, had obviously seen the approaching riders, for Free could see him moving toward the cottonwoods, Shorty Anson, the drive ramrod, in tow.

"What's the fuss?" Bose asked.

Free listened as Goodnight explained their situation to the mounted group.

"Free saw riders to our south and west. That could mean they aim to flank us. It might be nothing, but I've got too much invested in this drive to sit on my hands."

"What do you aim to do, Charlie?" Shorty asked.

"It looks like we might need to do a little scouting at sunset this evening," Goodnight answered. "Shorty, I'm going to take Bose and Free with me. We're going to find those riders Free saw. I don't think any of us can be at ease until we know who they are and what they're up to. You best stay and look over the herd. We can't afford to have us both out riding into who knows what."

Free felt a wave of pride spread across his chest. He felt useful, like every man ought to feel.

As the sun's last rays shone across the West Texas sky, Free rode slowly away from the main cattle herd and followed Goodnight's and Bose's leads. He maintained the back position as they crossed the Brazos in single file and headed up a small embankment on the far side of the river. Free kept a tight rein on his mount as the night promised a quarter moon, and he didn't want to be surprised by a low hanging limb or a Mexican ground squirrel burrow.

"Look for the glow or smoke of a fire," he heard

Goodnight whisper. "I'll feel a little better if I know this bunch is in their camp and not out scouting our herd. And remember we are upwind of the herd and hopefully downwind of those six riders. Once we are out of the herd's range, we might be able to hear voices from the rider's camp, so no talking, only hand signals from here on in."

Free nodded his head in understanding. He made sure he stayed within a saddle-length of his companions so their outlines remained visible in the darkness. A mile or so from the herd, he picked up the first sounds of the night. The words were unintelligible, but it was conversation from men. He saw Goodnight, riding the middle position, pull up his hand and form a fist. Free pulled back hard on Comida's reins at Goodnight's signal.

"Free," he heard Goodnight's raspy voice. "You and me are going to go on foot from here. Bose, you stay with the horses and be ready to help if things get cockeyed."

Free dismounted and handed his reins to Bose. He could see Goodnight's figure beginning a methodical walk toward a small rise ahead of them. The moon cast just enough light to shadow small mesquites and brush on the prairie. At the bottom of the rise, the conversation issuing from the camp became clear. Free followed Goodnight's lead, crouching low, inching his way to the top of the hill. At the top of the rise, he could see the orange glow of a fire illuminating the camp below.

"Free, I am going into the camp. You stay here and keep that Henry handy."

Free nodded a silent yes, then pulled the rifle up and placed it over his left arm. "Be careful, sir," he warned the trail boss.

Goodnight stood and started down the rise toward the camp below. "Hello the camp!"

A rush of activity became apparent in the camp, as Free could see men moving around frantically. He reckoned they were caught unaware.

"My name is Charles Goodnight. I'm driving a herd of long-horns to Cheyenne."

There was a moment of silence before a voice penetrated the darkness. Free turned his head toward the sound as the voice had a familiar ring to it. He couldn't identify it as to the speaker, but he had definitely heard it before. "Come on in, Mr. Goodnight. You are well known in these parts."

Chapter 9

Clear Fork Country, Texas 1868

Free lay on his stomach watching as Goodnight walked into the riders' camp. The cover of the night and a large clump of prairie grass, only twenty feet away, protected his position. He took a quick accounting of the six men now standing across from his trail boss. All appeared well heeled. With military precision, he moved the Henry across each of the men, sighting their positions in the event troubled boiled over. Even by campfire light, he could see they all carried the look of hard men. A brown mixture of dust and sweat painted their faces. Their tattered clothing showed the wear and tear of being on the run. He moved his eyes back and forth across the crew looking for any misstep and caught sight of a small, squat of a man stepping away from the bunch and toward Goodnight. The man's face was partially obstructed by his hat, hung low across his eyes. Free reckoned this man to be boss of the outfit. He moved the Henry's sights over the man's chest, his finger set lightly on the trigger. No matter what this outfit's story, Free knew they were up to no good.

"Come in, Mr. Goodnight." The stocky man reached toward the fire, pulling a pot from its edge. "Coffee?"

"Don't mind if I do." Goodnight kept his words friendly.

Free slowly closed his left eye and took aim down the Henry's barrel. He could see the five other men, ever so slowly, moving apart as Goodnight reached out to accept the offered coffee. Free kept his sight steady, his eye unblinking. Looking down the rifle barrel, he could see a half smile cross the boss's face. *Why does that smirk seem so familiar?* He tried to think back, but his concentration would not allow him to move his focus from the man.

The still night carried the conversation of the camp to where Free lay. "What brings you off the herd on a dark night, Mr. Goodnight?" The man leaned down and set the pot back into the fire's coals. "It seems a might dangerous."

Free noticed that Godnight had moved a little bit to his right giving him an unobstructed view of the boss. "Well, sir, I could hear conversation drifting with the wind and thought it might be polite to let you know we did have our herd downwind from you."

Free could see the wide smirk come across the stocky man's face once more. "You wanted to make sure none of us got soaked and began shooting our pistols?"

"I wasn't really thinking that far ahead," Goodnight replied. Free watched as the trail boss drank his coffee down in one gulp. "That's good coffee you boiled." Free wrapped his finger around the trigger as Goodnight handed the cup back to the man. "I just wanted to let you know where we were."

The man accepted the cup and handed it to one of the men behind him, never turning his back from Goodnight. "And where are my manners, Mr. Goodnight?" He moved forward and extended his hand. "I'm the law in this country. Me and the boys here have been following some thieves. The group has been rustling cattle off the Old Stone Ranch around Mule Creek. We lost their trail this afternoon near Fort Phantom Hill. I think they hightailed it to Mexico."

Free had never seen a lawman look the way this one did. He reckoned Mr. Goodnight had heard and seen enough, for he had begun to back out of the camp and into the shadows of the night. "I will thank you for the coffee and the conversation. Both were worth the ride out."

"It was a pleasure meeting you face to face, Mr. Goodnight. I wish you well on your journey to Wyoming."

Goodnight turned and started to walk back up the rise when the sheriff cleared his throat. Free kept the gun trained on the sheriff as the trail boss turned back toward the camp.

"We've also been tracking an ex-slave. A dangerous fellow. Seems he may have stolen some cattle himself. Might even be selling them to the Comanche. He was last seen around Jacksboro. You wouldn't have any opportunity to know of this man would you?"

"I wouldn't be able to say without knowing his name, sheriff," Goodnight replied.

"He goes by the name of Free Anderson."

Caught off guard at the mention of Free's name, Goodnight took a step back and stumbled against the slight incline of the hill. "No sir, I can't say that I have occasion to know that name."

Free saw the lawman's smirk change to an ugly frown, as if he knew Goodnight was lying. "Well, if you happen to run into him, let him know Sheriff

Jubal Thompson has a warrant to bring him in. Dead or alive."

Free rolled to his back, almost gasping aloud. In panic, he raised his eyes from the Henry and slid down the slope several feet. *Corporal Thompson!* That's where he remembered the smirk. The Palmito Ranch retreat was two years past, but he would never forget Jubal Thompson. And then Parks' last warning hauntingly came back to him. *Be careful Free; he's the sort to carry a grudge down a long road.*

Free stood next to Comida, tying his sleeping roll and belongings behind the horse's saddle. Several yards away, he could hear Goodnight and Bose engaged in what appeared to be a heated discussion. The fact that a local sheriff had accused one of their wranglers of rustling had to be foremost on their minds.

Free was still in shock over the realization that Jubal Thompson, now a lawman, seemed to be intent on settling an old grudge. He hated the thought of leaving the drive, but he couldn't see an opportunity to play his hand any other way. Somehow, he would have to prove his innocence, but he couldn't stay here and run the risk of being put into a jail under Jubal Thompson's control. At this moment, he was unsure of which way his path would lead, but his gut told him he needed to ride out.

"Free."

He turned and saw Goodnight walking toward him.

"We're up against it right now, Free."

Free could see the look of worry etched in Goodnight's forehead. "Don't worry sir, I won't cause you any further trouble. I've already made up my mind to ride out this evening."

"I appreciate the offer, Free, but don't be too hasty just yet. I have a plan."

"Mr. Goodnight, I thank you for all you've done for me. But if Jubal Thompson finds me riding with this herd, especially after you told him you didn't know of me . . . well, that could cost you everything. I can't do that to you or these men, sir."

"Free, I've run across all types of men in my life, and I can tell you straight up that this Jubal Thompson is a rattlesnake. I figure he is riding both sides of the law fence. But I do need for you to tell me everything about this man."

Free thought back to Boca Chica. He began to tell every detail he could remember of the crossing that night, plus the events at Fort Brown during the tribunal hearing. When he had finished, he shot a glance at Goodnight. "Now do you understand why I need to ride out. He's intent on revenge, and he's got the law on his shirt to accomplish it."

"I don't cater to bullies or lawbreakers, and I will protect my own, Free. Especially if they are innocent. A thief wearing a badge is still a thief."

Free looked at Godnight with great respect. "But to fight him right now would take every man. And to bring him down in a court could take time. How are you going to get the herd to Wyoming by the fall, if you're stuck in Texas helping me?" Free placed his right hand on the saddle horn and swung up on Comida. "It's not your trouble, sir."

Free felt Goodnight grab his boot. "Hold on, Free, and at least listen to me."

"That I'll do, Mr. Goodnight. I owe you that for sure."

"We're going to drive the herd to Wyoming. You included. And then we're all coming back here to take care of Jubal Thompson."

"I just don't see. . . ." Free looked down at the trail boss and shook his head back and forth. "How we're going to do that."

"I'm not saying it's going to be easy, but here's the plan. You're riding out tonight. Only instead of following our trail southwest, you're going to head north and west. That will get you to the New Mexico border much quicker. If you get a good start tonight, you should be able to reach the Kiowa Arroyo by morning."

Free now understood Goodnight's plan. "Ride through the Comancheria."

"That's the downside, Free. But if being an ex-slave ever had any value, it's now. Some of the Comanche are friendly to the black race. Personally I'd rather take my chances with the savages than the sheriff."

Free considered the plan. On short notice, he couldn't think of anything that carried better water. "So what happens if I reach the border?" he asked.

"When you reach the border," Goodnight corrected him, "you ride like the devil to Fort Sumner. It's a week's ride from here. I figure it'll take us a month with the herd. Just wait for us there. When we meet back up, we'll finish the drive to Cheyenne."

Free leaned from the saddle and stuck his hand out to Goodnight. "I am much in your debt, sir." He shook the trail boss' hand. "And I will make sure I repay that debt someday."

"You're a good man, Free. You owe me nothing. But I do want you to take this."

Free opened his hand as Goodnight passed a small cloth sack to him. "What is it, sir?"

"Payday. That's a month's advance. I don't like a man of mine riding alone without coin."

Free swallowed hard, choked with emotion, "Thank you, Mr. Goodnight." He pushed the sack into his boot. "And sir, I need to ask one more favor."

"What is it, Free?"

"If for some reason, any of this goes bad. I would appreciate you trying to reach a friend of mine and let him know how this all played out."

"Sure, son. What's his name?"

"He's known by Parks Scott. I figure any of the military posts along the southern plains can put you in touch with him. He supplies the cavalry with horses."

"I will do that, Free. Now you best get a wiggle on. This night is almost over."

Free held silence for a moment and then took spurs to Comida, riding away from Charles Goodnight and into the surrounding darkness.

Chapter 10

The Comancheria, Texas 1868

The West Texas heat shimmered across the blackened prairie grasses of the Comancheria. Wild fires had raged through this part of the plains some weeks earlier, burning several thousand acres. The southeast wind, a daily fixture here, was strangely absent this day, leaving even the toughest animals struggling for breath in the building humidity.

Parks sat on Horse in front of the only watering site for a hundred miles. The spring bubbled up to the ground from deep below the earth's surface. After the fire, it was easy to locate, for the grasses for several feet around the small hole were green and vibrant. A hundred yards to his south, he could see the herd of mustangs he had been trailing for days. The wild horses needed water, but Parks knew they would not venture forward as long as he guarded the spring.

Two weeks earlier, summoned to Fort Richardson by the officer in charge, Maj. James Hardin, he found The 6th Cavalry detachment in dire need of horses. A ration of corn acquired for horse feed had been poisonous and twenty of the cavalry's steeds had died in the previous month. The tragedy to the cavalry's horses was deplorable to Parks, but the opportunity to supply horses had come just as he had thought his business would go bust. Ever since the races at Fort Riley, he sat blacklisted as a supplier to the newly formed U.S. Cavalry. Although unspoken by the military, he knew whose signature dotted the bottom line of the order, and even though the lieutenant colonel had been court martialed soon after their encounter for leaving the field, getting the military to reverse the blacklisting was a bureaucratic muddle.

Before Major Hardin's request, Parks was preparing to go home and visit his mother. He reckoned she deserved to see her only son, but the job here offered a chance at redemption with the cavalry, and he hated to let this opportunity pass. He figured rounding up the full complement of horses might keep him in the Jacksboro settlement another two weeks. After that, he would head home to San Saba.

He studied the horses waiting in front of him and could see that the smell of water was strong, but the lead stallion, a solid buckskin, was not yet ready to drink. Parks called toward two of the settlement's soldiers. "One of you stay at the water. The other, follow me. We're going to take them around again." Parks let slack come to his reins and lightly tapped Horse's flank. "Let's move, Horse. This group doesn't seem to be ready yet." He spurred the pony forward, causing the mustangs to turn and set out to the east.

Over the past week, Parks and the soldiers had moved the mustangs in a great circle around the watering hole. He knew the animals were of a strong thirst, and they would not leave the area until they had an opportunity to drink. He was amazed at the mustangs' survival ability. Even after going four days without water, the ponies still carried sufficient energy to avoid the men trailing them.

The designated route the mustangs had chosen was a two-day loop around the spring. Each time they returned, a soldier guarded their path to the small watering area. Parks used an old Indian method of capture. When he saw signs that the lead stallion did not want to run the loop again, he removed the guard from the spring. The cool spring water settling in an exhausted mustang's belly would make the animal lethargic and unable to run at full strength, if at all. This is when the animal was vulnerable to roping.

"Mr. Scott, how long do you figure it will take to break them down?" The young soldier asked.

Parks looked over at the soldier. He could see that the private was merely a boy, probably not older than seventeen. "I can't say for sure; that buckskin stallion is still fairly strong. But if I were to guess, I would say another two days without water may have him where we want him." Parks shot another glance at the youth. The one real danger to this work was Indians. He didn't know if either of the two soldiers carried field experience with hostiles, but there was always the possibility of an encounter on this prairie. Bands of Comanche and Kiowa regularly scouted their land for intruders. Desperate for money, he had taken this job betting that the tribes had followed the buffalo away from the fire-ravaged land to the northern prairies of Indian Territory. So far, his bet had paid off. He thought once more of the two soldiers riding with him and prayed that his luck would continue to hold.

Following the mustang herd left a man with plenty of opportunity to think. Parks spent a portion of his time in the saddle counting the dollars from this capture. He figured twenty horses at sixty dollars a head would give him the needed funds to continue his business and maybe even hire some help. His thoughts carried to Free Anderson. When he had delivered the horses to Major Hardin, it just might be time to search out his old friend. There was no one he trusted more, and a partner might be the right fix for his business.

Chapter 11

The Kiowa Arroyo, Texas 1868

T he morning sun reflected with blinding intensity off a rock formation near the Salt Fork of the Brazos. Free could feel the heat radiating from the pitted sandstone walls as he traveled the almost dry riverbed. A metallic clang rattled through the air as Comida's shoes contacted the assorted sizes of pear-shaped river rock strewn through the sand. The riverbank, lined with willows, weaved through the land in a lazy, serpentine shape. Drawing Comida's rein to follow the next bend, he noticed a sand bar leading away from the river. With a flick of his spur, he turned Comida toward the bank, then rode across the sand and up a small hill of scrub oak. At the top of the incline, he looked down to a wide gully marking the leading edge of the Kiowa Arroyo.

The funnel-shaped draw held a tangle of greenbrier and cactus around its rim. Used by the Indians to run buffalo headlong to their deaths, the arroyo was a graveyard of bones. Over hardtack one night, Coyo had described the hunting technique at the arroyo. Several Kiowa warriors on ponies would stampede the buffalo down the funnel. At the arroyo's smallest point, the Indians constructed an earthen dam, reinforced with timber and rock. Once the bison piled into the dam at the back of the arroyo, they were trapped. From above,

Kiowa braves armed with spears and bows would slaughter the animals.

First sight of the arroyo sent a shiver down Free's spine. There was only one way in and one way out. His military training urged him to continue toward the border, away from this place. Surveying the top ledge, he realized it offered an unrestricted view of the canyon floor. This was the perfect place for an ambush.

Staring into the arroyo, he rubbed his chin and felt the stubble of a two-day-old beard. Travel-worn from the all night ride and contrary to his instinct, he decided the best place to remain out of sight was in the belly of the arroyo. Stepping from the stirrups, he pulled the reins forward over Comida's head. With great attentiveness, he looked around the top ledge once more before leading the horse down into the earthen gulch.

The funnel of the arroyo directed a cooling breeze through the floor of the ancient riverbed. At the back wall, Free found an old oak trunk with a large split down its center. He looked up and saw the bottom half of the tree still standing. He figured lightning had cleaved it in half. The twenty-foot section of the tree lying in the canyon floor was at least six feet around. He lifted Comida's saddle and set it over the log. The horse's back showed a line of white foam. He ran his hand over the entire length of the steed and in one motion threw the foam to the ground. "Go on, Comida," he spoke in a road weary voice. "Find some grass." The shade at the bottom of the arroyo still offered some green from the last of the winter grasses. The horse began to wander the arroyo, snipping at the ankle-high treat.

Satisfied as to Comida's care, Free took a small cloth from his saddlebag. Squirreled inside were three sourdough biscuits that he had stashed away for an emergency. Leaning back against the log, he set his hat on the ground next to him and un-wrapped the cloth. He took out the first biscuit and held it in front of his face. After three days in his saddle pack, the bread had taken on the ap-pearance of jerked beef. He bit down on the biscuit and pulled hard with his hand. The bread, with a texture similar to adobe, tasted as good as any-thing he had ever eaten. He lifted the canteen from around his saddle horn and took a long swallow of water. Comfortable, he eased back against the log. Within seconds, he felt the weariness of his body forcing his eyelids slowly down.

A series of rapid snorts brought Free's eyes open with a start. He took a minute to regain his bear-ings and then looked over to the horse. Comida's tail was brushing flies off his back while he contin-ued to eat grass. Free yawned and stretched his arms away from his body. "How long have I been out?" Yawning once more, he rose and dusted his chaps. "What I wouldn't give for a bath and a shave right now." He spoke aloud, twisting his neck back and forth. He reckoned it would be foolish to waste any more time in the arroyo as Jubal could be close on his trail. Walking toward Comida, he noticed the horse mouthing his bit. The sound of teeth on metal made him uneasy. "We better light out, Co-mida." Picking up the reins dragging the ground, he rubbed the horse's forehead. "We best get our-selves out of the sheriff's reach and into New Mex-ico as Mr. Goodnight advised."

Free saddled Comida and retied his bedroll. He looped the canteen back around the saddle horn and then pulled himself up on his horse. Rested, his mind began to think again. He worried about his mother and earning enough money to build her a house. He hoped he could clear his good name, and most of all he wondered as to Jubal Thompson's whereabouts.

Then he heard the click. He knew the sound. It was a sound that any man easily recognizes no matter when or where it might occur. The sound of a bullet being chambered into a Henry .44, followed by the cocking of a rifle lever.

"Well lookey what we got here," he heard a man's voice echo around the top of the arroyo. "Just like you said, Jubal, the colored done skedaddled from the trail drive with his tail between his legs."

At the top of the arroyo, Free could just make out six figures standing around the ledge. This bunch knew what they were doing, for they had him looking directly into the sun. There was no way he could draw and get off a shot without suffering a hail of lead from above.

"Sergeant!"

Free had no doubt as to who owned the voice.

"If it were me, Sergeant, I'd drop the Colt and step down from the horse."

The click of four more Henrys, cocked in unison, told Free he had better do what the man said. He pulled the Colt from the waistband of his pants and let it fall to his feet.

"Now step down, or I'll shoot you off that horse like a dog!"

Free was angry for allowing himself to be in such a situation, but he knew there was nothing to do but dismount Comida. He hoped it wasn't the last thing he ever did.

Wishing he had never stopped at this place, Free faced the mouth of the canyon at the instruction of the lone rider left atop the gully's rim. The remaining five were making their way down the funnel. A smirking Jubal Thompson held the lead.

Unsure as to his best course, he spied Mr. Goodnight's Henry set in his saddle ring. He might have chance against the five riders with the gun. The fallen oak would certainly provide enough cover. Free moved quickly, grabbing Comida's reins and turning the horse's body between him and the approaching riders. He reached for the Henry, pulling it halfway from the saddle ring when the dirt near his boots dusted up, followed by the echo of a rifle shot.

"Leave that Henry in the ring, Sergeant!"

Free released the rifle at the sound of a shell being ejected and raised his hands to the sky. He turned and saw the sixth rider's rifle aimed at his chest.

"That wasn't too smart," Jubal said.

He stood in silence as the five circled him, enclosing him in a wall. A shiver of fear crept up his backbone and caused his shoulders to quiver ever so slightly. He had experienced the same shiver before every battle during his war years. The one thing he knew from those years was that a man bundled in fear did not make rational decisions. He breathed deep, hoping to relax his tension, but the sight of five white men surrounding him in the middle of the Comancheria did little for his anxiety.

Jubal Thompson sat directly to his front, leaning on his saddle horn and staring down at him. Free could see a smug look of satisfaction beaming from his face.

"Sergeant, is that guilt I see set on your face?"

Free kept his focus straight ahead, refusing to look Jubal in the eye. He figured he didn't need to anger these men any further.

"Well boys, it appears that for once, Sergeant Anderson has lost his voice. Too bad he didn't lose it that evening at Boca Chica."

Free shot a glance toward Jubal. The realization that it didn't matter if he spoke or kept quiet came over him. Whatever he said or did not say carried no weight. These men aimed to do him harm either way. He could feel the anger rising inside of him. "No, I can speak, Sheriff."

"By your tone, I figure you haven't learned your lesson. It seems a colored in your situation might learn to be a bit more respectful of a white man."

Free felt the heat of anger warming his chest and face. "I'm a freedman, Jubal. Don't mistake that!"

"That's mighty big talk for a cattle thief accused of selling stolen beeves to the Indians."

"You know that's a lie!" Free shouted. He eyed the men around him, trying to calculate the odds of reaching his pistol lying on the ground beneath his feet.

"I see that look, Sergeant. I would forget about that pistol of yours. You'll be shot to pieces before you can even thumb the hammer. But by all means, let her fly if you think the best of it."

Free knew the chances of getting off even one shot were slim. But now he reckoned that if Jubal wanted him dead today, they would have shot him from the ledge. In his mind that bought some time for thinking. "You have no proof for any of your trumped up charges, Jubal."

"I don't know, Sergeant, what's a runaway slave doing in the middle of the Comanche range by himself? It would appear he's here to meet with the savages. By the way, my man up top there has a string of stolen cattle we supposedly took off of you. I think we might have plenty of needed proof."

Free kept his gaze forward and his eyes emotionless. He cursed to himself as the sheriff's laugh echoed throughout the arroyo. From the corner of his eye, he watched as the rider closest to him stepped down from his horse. The man stood at least six foot four and appeared to be the lead rider. The tall rider reached down and picked up the discarded pistol from the ground.

"Johnny," he heard Jubal speak to the man. "Get him on his horse and tie his hands to the saddle."

From above, the sixth rider called out.

"Jubal! Kiowa are heading down stream!"

Chapter 12

The Kiowa Arroyo, Texas 1868

F ree worked to pull his hands free of the rawhide string binding him to his saddle. The man called Johnny held a rope around Comida's neck leading the animal off the canyon floor.

Outside of the gulch, ten Kiowa warriors sat on multi-colored ponies. Free looked on in wonder as Jubal rode out toward the warriors. He carried both hands palm up as he greeted the Kiowa.

He remembered Mr. Goodnight telling stories about the Kiowa and how the Comanche and the Kiowa had been fierce enemies for centuries, fighting over the buffalo ranges. But as more whites moved West, the tribes had joined together in the common cause of raiding settlers, stealing horses and taking lives. The fact that ten Kiowa braves sat talking to Jubal had him stumped as to the reason.

They spoke for several minutes, and then Jubal pointed to his right. Free followed his motion and watched as the sixth rider pushed the twenty or so longhorns toward the Kiowa.

He noticed the Kiowa leader motion across his chest and then push his right hand toward Jubal, mimicking the lever action of a repeating rifle. Their dealings apparently completed, the warriors moved the cattle toward the riverbed and quietly disappeared into the land.

Confused, Free took note as Jubal turned and shot a gaze his way.

"Well, Sergeant, there's our proof. It looks like to me and my deputies that we just caught you selling stolen cattle to the savages."

Free looked around at the outfit, their faces all gleamed with laughter. If he was going to survive any of this, he had better learn as much as possible about Jubal's dealings with the Kiowa. "Nobody's going to believe I rustled twenty head by myself, rode into the Comancheria alone, and sold them to Kiowa braves." He looked at the deputies and hoped he had planted some doubt in their heads. If so, he might get Jubal to explain more of his plan.

"Don't listen to this ex-slave, boys." A streak of blackness flashed in Jubal's eye. "I'll bet that other ex-slave, Bose Ikard, is in on it with him. I'll bet you they're both dealing with the savages. Hell, the whole trail drive outfit may be working with him."

And that was it. Free knew if he pushed any further, he could bring Mr. Goodnight, Bose, and the rest of the drivers down with him. Jubal had put a spoke in the wheel, and he knew there was no one left to help.

"Now, you might think about hobbling that lip of yours, Sergeant, or you'll be riding shank's mare back to the Flats.

Free stared through crusted eyes as he plodded behind the six riders into The Flats. His tongue felt swollen, and blood oozed from the corner of his mouth. Small black gnats tormented his battered lips and eyes, continually swarming his face. With his hands tied to the saddle horn, there was little he could do for relief but shake his head, momentarily disrupting the pests. For the past two days, he had existed on several pulls of water from his canteen. Jubal had given him just enough water to keep him alive for the journey into town.

His body ached with a dull pain that throbbed with every beat of his heart. And for each step Comida took on the rough, uneven land, a shot of lightning struck his temple. Before leaving the arroyo, the man Jubal called Johnny had used a leather strap tied with tiny slivers of flint to soften him up. "Keep you from having any stupid thoughts on your way to the jail house," he remembered the man telling him. As they approached The Flats, his shirt was little more than shredded cloth.

As Comida trudged through the street, Free noticed a girl standing to his left. He leaned over, squinting at the figure. He wanted to tell her he was innocent. That he had been framed. But the girl simply stared at him as the riders passed. Leaning back, he kept his stare on the figure, certain he had seen sadness in her eyes.

Somewhere far off, he heard a voice asking for water.

"Johnny, shut him up!"

Free felt the sting of a rawhide string wrap around his neck. "Shut-up, Sergeant! You want to make the town's people think we're curly wolves!"

Free felt tears well up in his eyes, and a hopelessness he had never experienced before settled over him. As a lone tear dropped to his cheek, he realized the sheriff was parading him through town as a whipped dog. Jubal wanted everyone to see the ex-slave crying like a baby on his way to jail.

Furious and determined to remove the cloud of doubt entrenched in his mind, he closed his eyes and conjured up memories locked deep in his head. Rising to his consciousness, he saw the painful vision of his father falling in the field, the pitiful sight of his mother toiling alone in Missouri, and the horrific sight of soldiers dying at Boca Chica. Every muscle in his body tensed, and he tasted blood in his mouth. Licking the liquid with his tongue, he realized he had bitten a hole in his lip. Pushing his back straight, he willed himself to ride tall. *Act like a freedman*, he reminded himself, and staring ahead to his captors, he muttered, "We'll see who ends up dead."

Chapter 13

The Flats, Texas 1868

The Flats' jail cell was stark, located outdoors and giving the prisoners little protection from the West Texas heat, blowing sand and the at-times relentless humiliation of the town's people. The stand-alone stone cell was six feet tall and six foot square. Small vertical slits in the rock allowed for light and air. The door, made from a latticework of iron, used a Hobbs lock to keep the prisoners secure.

Jubal had made it plain to all that he did not want to see or smell the drunks, coloreds, and Indians who would occupy his jail.

As Jubal and the riders approached the far end of town, he noticed Deputy Von Riggins standing outside the jail.

"Howdy, Sheriff." Von called out.

Jubal acknowledged the deputy with a nod of his head. "Get out here and help us!" he yelled as he stepped down from his horse. He allowed the deputy to pass him before he walked toward the west side of the building where the cell was located.

"Where'd he come from?" Jubal yelled out to his deputy. He was looking at a large, passed out individual. The man wore a buffalo scalp on his head, complete with a full set of horns.

"He's a buffalo hunter, Jubal." The deputy shot back. "Came into town last night shooting up the place with a shotgun."

"Well, get him out of here before I shoot the two of you!" Jubal watched in anger as the deputy ran back from the dirt street.

"I thought I was supposed to help the riders?" Von mumbled.

"You're supposed to do what I tell you!" Jubal kicked at the drunk. "Is Judge Freemont still at the Fort?" He looked on as two of his riders dragged Free into the outdoor cell and dumped his body on the only item in the cage, a stained mattress set on the dirt. The mattress carried the signature of all the drunks who had lain there in preceding days. Even outdoors and with the accompanying West Texas wind, the cell smelled rank and stifling. "One of you get some water from the horse trough and put it in there with him. I don't want him dying on me before I hang him." He turned his attention back to his deputy, watching as Von deposited the buffalo hunter half into the street and half onto the boardwalk.

"I think he's set to leave today, Jubal. I believe he said he was heading out to Weatherford to hold court."

Jubal looked at Free, passed out in a heap. "At least he won't be any trouble for the rest of the day." He rubbed his neck and looked back to Von. "Get over to the Fort and tell him he's not to leave today. I have a case that needs trying, and it won't wait for the next circuit. I need to see him today."

"But, Jubal," The deputy appeared anxious. "The judge ain't gonna like that."

"Just tell him what I said!" Jubal set a hard gaze on the deputy. "Tell him now!" His steel eyes bore through the deputy. He kept his stare until Von turned and ran down the boardwalk toward Fort

Griffin. "And the rest of you," Jubal looked to his riders, "we've still got work to do. Johnny, you come with me. And you five," He gestured at the others. "Get yourselves some grub over at the Jenkins House. Tell the old man to put it on the town's tab and have him send two plates over to the sheriff's office with plenty of coffee."

Jubal motioned for Johnny to follow and started walking to the front of the jail, still speaking to the five as he walked off. "And boys, get your fill, because as soon as Johnny and I are done, you're heading out again."

Inside his office, he slammed the jail keys on his desk and walked around to his chair. The room was a small ten by twenty rectangle with canvas lining the walls. "We've got to move those cattle to New Mexico by the end of the week," he said to Johnny. "Everything has come off real grand for us, but I don't like tempting fate. We've been lucky to hold the Kiowa off with the promise of repeaters, but they'll come to their senses before too long." He reached into a side drawer on his desk and pulled out a bottle of whiskey. "They're holding over a thousand head of ours, and I'm getting a touch uneasy about that."

"Those cattle would already be in New Mex if we hadn't spent the last two weeks chasing down that sergeant of yours," Johnny said.

Jubal felt a spark of anger in his chest. "That sergeant of mine, as you call him, is our alibi! And the sooner I get Judge Freemont to try him, the sooner he'll hang! And when he does hang, we won't need to be looking over our shoulders worrying if we're all going to be found out! Now does that make sense to your feeble little mind? Or do I need to explain it some more? Don't you worry about that sergeant of mine! You've got one job and only one job! You worry about getting those cattle to New Mexico and getting our money!"

"Aw right, Jubal. Just calm down. I understand. But we've been riding for almost two weeks. The boys and I could all use a bath and a shave."

Jubal rose, turned, and kicked his chair away from him, slamming it into the wall behind him. "I don't give a continental what you and the boys want!" He let his hand drop slowly to the butt of his Colt. "Those cattle are going to be moved this week!"

He made a mental note of Johnny's reluctance to do as told. "If you want to make the decisions, Johnny, you know what to do!" Jubal threw a glance toward Johnny's holster. "But I hope you understand I'm not some tied-up runaway slave before you skin that leather!"

"Simmer down, Jubal. I'm not challenging you. But me and the boys aren't slaves either. You best remember that. We've got our breaking points too."

Jubal reached behind and pulled his chair back under him. He looked at the man sitting across from him and gave thought to shooting him on the spot. But he knew he needed six men to help deal with the Kiowa. It would take every one of them to kill T`on-syan and his warriors and then move the cattle to New Mexico. But most of all, he needed all six to take the fall for the thousand head of rustled cattle. The six would all be dead before they returned to The Flats. The thought drew a smile to his face. "You're right, Johnny," He pushed the bottle across his desk. "Take a drink. When we've eaten, you and the boys can clean up and let off some steam. But you need to be out of here by sun-up tomorrow."

He watched as Johnny reached for the bottle, his face all grin. "Thanks, Jubal, we'll get this done for you."

The Sheriff nodded and then added. "One more thing, I need for you to bring back one hide from those cattle we left with the Kiowa yesterday. Make sure you have enough hide to show the brand. That's our evidence against the sergeant outside. If I know T`on-syan, he's already butchered at least one of those steers."

"Maybe all of them. T'on-syan and his bunch are lucky the Comanche haven't killed them all by now."

"Well, that's worked in our favor for sure. It's a good thing the Comanche don't have an interest in the staked plains just yet." Jubal rose and crossed to the front of his desk. He motioned for the bottle and took a big drink. "Because if they did, T`on-syan and his renegades would all be dead by now. I don't think the Comanche take kindly to Indians working with whites."

"What do I tell T`on-syan when he wants to see their rifles?"

Jubal rocked back in his chair. He held the whiskey bottle tight to his chest and seemed momentarily lost in thought. "You open up on them, Johnny. You kill every one of them. Understood?" He took another pull from the bottle and handed it back to the cowboy.

"Understood."

A knock brought Jubal's attention back toward the jailhouse door. "Food's here. Let her in."

From the open door, a young colored girl entered the room. Head down, she scurried over to Jubal's desk, placing a wicker basket on top. "Clara," He spoke with little respect. "What are we eating today?"

"Mr. Jenkins sent beef steak, beans, and biscuits."

Jubal watched as she set two tin plates of food on the desk. "And how about our coffee?"

"Oh yes, Sheriff, I have coffee too." She lifted a silver pot from the basket with two tin cups tied by string to the handle." Can I get you anything else, Sheriff?"

That'll do right now, Clara. You best get back to the hotel. But you be here first thing tomorrow morning to get my wash. Understood?"

"Yes sir. I'll be here first thing."

Jubal watched the young girl leave, and then he and Johnny began digging into their plates.

After filling his belly, Jubal looked toward Johnny. "Now remember, when you boys get to New Mexico with the cattle, the Mexicans don't get so much as a look at them until you see the money."

"I know what to do, Jubal. You've told me a hundred times already."

"And I'll tell you a hundred more times if need be. I don't want any of you boys missing your cut of the loot because a Mexican put a .44 in your gut." Jubal untied the cups from the coffee pot handle and poured them both full. He pushed one cup of the black liquid toward Johnny and drank from the other himself. "They will try to ambush you for the cattle. Just be certain you understand that."

"I know, Jubal. I know. We take the money, and then we lead the Mex's to the valley where the cattle are grazing."

Jubal uncorked the whiskey once more and

poured a shot into his coffee tin. "That's good, Johnny. Real good. And remember after you show them the cattle, you kill them too. All of them. Understood?"

"Don't worry, Jubal, when we ride back to The Flats, we'll be leaving a heap of dead Indians and Mexicans in our dust."

That's good, Johnny, Jubal smiled to himself, *cause when this is all over, you'll be dead, and I'll be in Mexico with twenty thousand dollars.*

A bothersome wetness dripped down Free's nose and onto his lips. With great effort, he pushed his eyes open to harsh daylight. He blinked several times, trying to clear his confusion. Above the ringing in his ears, he heard a woman's voice speaking rapidly.

"Sir? Are you OK?"

He pushed up on his right elbow and lifted his head and chest toward the sound. "What?" A dryness of sand and blood lined his mouth and throat, causing him to flick his tongue repeatedly in an attempt to raise enough spit to swallow.

"Are you OK?"

A girl, maybe all of eighteen, was talking to him. "What?" He pointed to his ears. "I can't hear anything but ringing." He placed his hand to his nose and could see that the wetness was water.

"I dripped some water down your face to wake you," she said and then pushed the water bucket toward him. "I'm sorry, but if the sheriff catches me here, he'll beat me with a strap."

Free caught a whiff of the water and grabbed the bucket. He turned it upside down, pouring as much water down his front as in his mouth.

"Don't drink too much too fast. You'll get the cramps."

The girl removed a piece of beefsteak from the basket she held.

"Here, eat this."

He grabbed the meat from the girl's hand in so fierce a manner that he noticed she recoiled. "I'm sorry," he spoke in a loud tone. "But I haven't eaten in three days."

"I watched them bring you in today. What did you do?"

Free pulled up against the cell door and leaned his right shoulder against the bars to support his body. "It's something that happened a long time ago. Between me and the sheriff." He fixed a long gaze into the young girl's eyes. "What's your name?"

"Clara Mason."

"Clara Mason." He rolled the name around in his head. "Was that you in the street this morning? I thought I saw my mother, but that was you. Wasn't it? I thought I was dreaming."

"Yes, that was me."

"Well, Clara, I think you might have saved my life." After the few bites of protein and water, he could feel his head begin to clear. He saw the girl drop her eyes downward but could make out a small smile appear at the corners of her mouth. "I was feeling ready to throw up the sponge just a while ago." He pushed one hand through his cage and felt Clara's hand. "I owe you. Now you best leave before the sheriff comes out here."

"I don't know your name."

"Free. Free Anderson."

He watched Clara stand. She was slender and

small but stood with a silent grace. "Go on, Clara. Get out of here."

"I'll bring you more food tonight when it's dark, Free Anderson."

Aware of the fleeting moment, his gaze held her beauty as his mind stumbled for any reason to call her back. "Clara! Wait!" he cried out. "One more thing." He watched her toss a look toward the street and then turn back to the cell. "I might need more than just food from you."

"What do you mean?"

He searched her eyes and with some reluctance asked, "Could you go to the Fort on my behalf? If I aim to make it out of this mess alive, I'm going to need some outside help, and right now the army is all the family I can claim."

"I'll do what I can, Free. But I don't hold much better standing than you at the Fort."

"I understand. But it's a chance. And right now I'll take any chance I can."

He watched her eyes soften, yielding to his request. "OK, Free, I'll try. I know what it's like without anyone to turn to."

"Thank you, Clara." He leaned his head against the cool steel of the cell door, his hands wrapped through the latticework of metal. "Thank you. I'll let you know when the time is right."

He felt her touch on the back of his hand.

"Don't worry. I'll do all I can."

Rejuvenated, he watched her turn away, hurrying into the streets of The Flats. As she vanished from sight, he fell back to the mattress thinking. *With Clara's help and the food, I'm holding two aces in my hand. Two aces that Jubal doesn't know a thing about.*

* * *

Jubal stood outside of his office with one foot on the hitching post. He poked at his boot with a seven-inch knife blade and flicked pieces of dried earth onto the ground. Taking a glance down the wide main street that ran the length of The Flats, he saw Judge Freemont moving toward him, his gait purposeful.

"Jubal! What in the hell is going on?"

Jubal took his boot from the post and dusted his dungarees. "Well hello to you too, Judge Freemont."

"Don't play games with me, Jubal. I'm supposed to be in Weatherford in three days."

"What's going on there? A drunken cowboy shoot someone's prize pig?" Jubal laughed. "I've got an important case here that needs to be tried." He stepped down onto the street and stood eyeball to eyeball with the judge. He knew the judge to be from the old hard-line faction of Texans, a man who believed slaves were property of their owners no matter what Washington said. "I've got a thieving runaway slave selling cattle to the Comanche." He saw his words caught the judge's attention. "He rustled cattle from the Old Stone Ranch."

"A slave, you say?"

"A runaway." Jubal added. "And a savage collaborator."

"Why didn't you just say so, Sheriff. Is he ready for trial?"

"Pretty much." Jubal looked away from the judge and stared down the street. "I'm sending my riders out tomorrow morning to pick up some of the hides the Comanche left behind. They should show the brand that he sold them."

"That's a good idea, Jubal, but I've heard all I

need to in this matter. Have your man ready for trial first thing tomorrow. I want to be heading to Weatherford by mid-morning."

Jubal flashed a quick smile. "Don't worry, he'll be ready."

"And, Sheriff . . . make sure you and the slave are presentable in my courtroom."

"Not to worry." Jubal looked down at his shirt. "We'll both be washed." As the circuit judge departed, Jubal laughed to himself, *Lucky for me that Judge Freemont is more a stickler for decorum than the law.*

Chapter 14

The Flats, Texas 1868

The raucous crowing of a rooster beckoned The Flats to life. Awake for hours, Free stood in the doorway of the ever-shrinking cell, his gaze centered on the Jenkins House. He waited with great restlessness for Clara to appear. During the night, she had carried biscuits and beefsteak to him, and the victuals were speeding his body's healing. Functioning with a clear mind, he came to realize the enormity of his situation. It was the word of an ex-slave against the word of the town's sheriff. In his boot, he felt the six coins Mr. Goodnight had given him pressed against his ankle. Undaunted by the overwhelming odds stacked against him, he figured the money might help him gain an edge before the sheriff's fandango played out.

Across the street, he observed Clara making her way to the jail, wicker basket in hand. Crossing the thoroughfare, she avoided eye contact, but he knew she was aware of his gaze. He watched as she stepped up on the boardwalk and then disappeared from view. *If I survive all of this, Clara Mason, I would like to call on you.*

Minutes later Jubal appeared with Clara following, a wooden pail in her arms.

"Sergeant, Clara here has brought you a wash bucket filled with cold water and plenty of soap."

Clara set the bucket in front of his cell door.

Jubal unlocked the padlock on the door and sloshed the bucket toward him.

"She's going over to the dry goods store to get you a new shirt and pants. Make sure you're finished washing by the time she returns."

Free made note that the sheriff was dressed in a newly pressed white shirt and clean woolen trousers. "What's going on, Jubal?"

"Your trial is what's going on, Sergeant, and Judge Freemont wants you bathed. He doesn't care much for the smell of your kind."

Free reckoned his would be a very short trial. His time as a freedman had been harsh, but educating. To survive the days ahead, he knew he couldn't think like a shave tail anymore. "How does my kind smell, Sheriff?"

He noticed the smirk of superiority form on Jubal's face. Roused to anger by the long days and nights in his cramped stone confinement, he vowed to wipe that smirk from the sheriff's face before this affair ended.

"By the way, Sergeant, new clothes cost money. I'm going to sell your horse and saddle before the trial to pay for your wardrobe and your court costs."

"You can't do that, Jubal! There's no judgment against me! And the law has no right to a man's horse!"

"Well, unless you have some coin, that's exactly what I'm going to do. And if you have any complaints, Sergeant, you can tell them to the Judge when you see him."

"Why are you doing all this, Jubal? We fought on the same side at Palmito Ranch. Why do you hate me so?"

The sheriff's eyes went black, dulling their brightness into a darkness of hate.

"I'm doing this because you got uppity, Sergeant! You think I don't know that you and your friend Parks set me up for Boca Chica. Did you really think I would just lie down while the army drummed me out as a non-commissioned officer? You made your play, and now I'm making mine. And when this is all over and you're swinging from a rope, we'll see who held the best string!"

Free now understood the mount he saddled. He hoped the sheriff's unbridled hate might force him into a mistake. He reminded himself to keep his mind focused for that moment. He walked the length of his stone prison several times, letting his options play out in his head. Knowing Comida was crucial to any escape attempt, he stopped pacing and looked out the cell door to Jubal. "I've got money."

Jubal leaned against the iron door and smiled. "Clara, you best get back to the hotel. And don't forget my laundry inside the office."

Free locked stares with Clara and nodded west toward Fort Griffin. As she vanished around the corner, he threw his gaze back to Jubal. "I'll give you gold coin; just leave my horse be."

"You're not really in any position to barter right now Sergeant. Let me see your money."

Free reached into his boot and pulled out the cloth sack. He removed two coins and placed them in the sheriff's outstretched hand. The prospect of losing the money grated on him, but he knew if he did catch a break, he had to have Comida available. He watched with careful interest as Jubal studied the coins. When the sheriff looked up again, he stuck an arm through the bars, his palm up.

"All of it, Sergeant. Give me all of it, or that horse goes to the livery stable to be sold."

Enraged, Free curled his lip in anger. Without a word, he handed the cloth sack to the grinning Jubal Thompson.

"Walk!"

Free could feel the long barrel of a Henry .44 pressed hard into his spine. Using the rifle as a ramrod, Von Riggins was marching him from the jail to the Jenkins House. He shuffled in small strides, his movement restricted by the shackles binding his hands and feet. Forced to walk in a series of quick, small steps, he could hear the heavy clang of the chains as they hit against one another.

He noticed a small group of citizens lining the boardwalk and watching the morning spectacle. He could feel their stares as they looked at him with curious faces. Looking west, he directed his attention at the far end of town, hoping for any sign of Clara. He prayed she had made her way safely up the bluff to Fort Griffin.

At the hotel front, he noticed the six riders from the arroyo mounting their horses. He shot a hard glare at the lead man, Johnny.

"Well lookey at the sergeant, boys. He done got his self a new set of clothes." Johnny laughed. "I don't blame you though; those other clothes of yours were just rags."

Free cast a hard gaze to the faces of the laughing men. Anger rising, he took a step toward Johnny, only to feel the barrel of the Henry come down on his shoulder. The steel caused a streak of heat to radiate up his neck. He winced in pain and stared into Johnny's eyes. "Laugh while you can cowboy," he muttered in a cold voice.

"You gonna be hanging around long, Sergeant?" Johnny asked.

"Get going!" He heard Von mumble. "Or I'll whop you again!"

Free shuffled onto the boardwalk and held a steady gaze on the six as they rode west away from The Flats. He took several deep breaths to calm himself. Figuring an ambush awaited him in the courtroom; he knew keeping his wits was essential in avoiding a tree branch today.

Regardless of his present circumstance, the cold bucket bath had been a godsend. Jubal had used it as one more way to show his control. But for Free, it served to strengthen his resolve. More importantly, it made him think. And his thoughts told him not one church stood in The Flats. Sending Clara to Fort Griffin, after she delivered his clothes was the smart play, as he was a decorated war hero honorably mustered out of the service. But if no one at the Fort listened, he had yet another card to play. A card he hoped could buy him a little more time from Jubal's rush to a hanging.

Entering the hotel dining room, Free made note that only the judge and Jubal were present. Judge Freemont sat at a round table with papers spread across its top. The deputy halted him several feet in front of the makeshift judge's bench. He looked on with a steadiness of mind as the judge addressed him.

"Sir, do you understand the charges against you today?"

He felt Von push the rifle further into his back.

"Yes sir. But I want the judge to know-." The slamming of the judge's hand on the table startled Free, interrupting him mid-stream.

"The prisoner will answer only the questions asked by this court. He will not engage in dialogue of his own unless asked to do so. Now, sir, what is your plead?"

Once again, he felt the gun bump his back. "Not guilty, Judge."

"Very well. Sheriff Thompson, do you promise to tell the whole truth in the matter before this court?"

Free watched Jubal turn his way before answering, the ever-inciting smirk present on his face.

"I do, Judge."

"In the matter of the county against Free Anderson, what can you testify to?"

"Judge, myself and the riders gathered information that Free Anderson was rustling cattle off the Old Stone Ranch and selling the beeves to the Indians."

Free could see there would be little truth in this court. Now it appeared that the judge was in deep with Jubal.

"That's a lie!"

"Deputy."

Free felt a sharp jab from the Henry's barrel. Grimacing, he watched the judge's face contort in anger.

"If the prisoner interrupts this proceeding again, you will take him back to his cell until we have finished this matter. Now proceed, Sheriff."

"We trailed him to the Kiowa Arroyo near New Mexico. We observed him selling the beeves to Indians. After the savages departed, we captured him and brought him back to the jail."

Free watched as the judge looked up. "Sir, this is a most grievous crime. Collaboration with savages and rustling are hanging offenses in this territory and in my court. Therefore, it is this court's judgment that you hang by the neck until dead. The sentencing will be carried out at a time and place to be determined by Sheriff Thompson."

Free felt no shock or surprise. He watched as the judge stood and placed his papers in a flat case.

"Judge, I request a preacher be present at my hanging."

"What was that?"

Free remained calm as Judge Freemont brought his head up from the table. His facial expression conveyed a look of confusion as to the petition.

"I believe I am entitled a preacher to pray for me and hear my last words before I hang."

He watched as the judge and Jubal stared at one another. Both were caught off guard by his request.

"Sir, we do not have a preacher in The Flats."

As the judge turned back, Free noticed a look of astonishment on his face. In the same instant, the rifle barrel moved away from his back.

"I would suggest you find one."

The voice from behind didn't belong to Von. Curious, Free shot a glance over his left shoulder and glimpsed the blue color of a cavalry uniform with lieutenant's bars showing. He turned back toward Jubal. The sheriff's face wrinkled hard at the forehead.

"What is your business here, lieutenant?" the judge asked.

"You mean the army's business, your honor. This man is a decorated soldier of rank. I am here to see he receives fair and just treatment."

"You understand, lieutenant that you have no jurisdiction over this court?"

"I understand, Judge. But I hope you understand that if this man wants a preacher, you have an obligation to provide such. If not, I will file a report with the government that a territory judge would not allow a decorated war hero to have counsel with a preacher before he left this earth."

Free exhaled in relief, figuring he had bought himself a little more time.

"You can't do that, Judge; you know the Jacksboro preacher travels afoot!" Jubal shouted.

Free observed the lieutenant had moved up even with him. From the corner of his mouth, he spoke in hushed tone. "The Indians will let the preacher pass, but if he's on horseback, they'll take his mount. Rumor has it that he lost six horses before he got wise."

"The army can't tell this town how it should enforce the law!" Jubal pleaded.

"Don't push it, Jubal. The last thing you want is trouble with the army right now," the lieutenant offered.

"Sheriff," the judge interrupted. "A supply line is riding to Fort Richardson this morning. I will ask them to get the preacher heading here immediately."

"But, Judge."

Free could sense Jubal's frustration. The sheriff did not want to wait one second to put him on the noose.

"That might take a week or more."

"What's the hurry, Sheriff? This man can hang seven days from now and still be just as dead as if you hanged him today. That is this court's decision."

As the Judge walked past, Free turned toward

his benefactor. "I appreciate your coming to help me, Lieutenant."

"You served your country when needed, Sergeant. I think your country can return the favor."

Free felt the wrist irons pressing hard against his flesh. He spun to see Jubal pulling on the metal cuffs, a noticeable flush of red set onto his face.

"Excuse me, Lieutenant," Jubal interrupted. "This prisoner needs to get back to his cell."

"Sheriff, the army will require a reporting on this man. If you don't mind, I need to spend some time with him to obtain the necessary information for Washington."

"You can talk to him all you want, Lieutenant, but across the street in his cell. The law says I'm to keep him there until he hangs."

"Very well, Sheriff, I'll walk over with you." The lieutenant towered in height over Jubal and looked down on him with a scowl. "I know how you abide the law."

Back in his cell, Free rubbed his wrists, glad to be out of his restraints. Jubal snapped the padlock to his cell shut and then left him and the lieutenant. "How does a man like Jubal Thompson get to be sheriff of a town?" Free looked toward the lieutenant.

"First things first. My name is Lieutenant Joseph Swafford."

Free thrust his hand through the door, "A pleasure, Lieutenant. I go by the name Free Anderson. I was a sergeant in the 62nd Colored Infantry during the war."

"Glad to meet you, Sergeant Anderson. Now to your question. Fort Griffin is a relatively new fort. And The Flats here sprung up almost overnight.

But it's growing everyday, and I imagine will be a boomtown in short order. Not only does the location offer the fort for commerce, but it sits on a crossroad for trail drives and stage lines. And with a military presence now established, it can't be too long before buffalo hunters follow the great herds' southern migration. Our mutual friend Jubal recognized that and brought in several of his war friends just as the town was starting up. I believe he calls them "The Riders." He talked up his war service and promised the businesses and local ranchers that he would take no salary for working, only a portion of the fines he levied against lawbreakers. As you can imagine, a sheriff who had a war record, and was in effect working for free, was too much to pass up for a fledgling township."

"And the army lets him do as he pleases?"

"Believe me, Sergeant, we keep our hands full just trying to keep the Comanche and Kiowa from raiding between our post-war fort line. The Indians might be more disobliged if we could keep the white settlers off their prairies. But more of them show up everyday. And all of them expect protection from hostiles across thousands of acres of open range."

"I understand, Lieutenant, and I'm not trying to say my trouble is your worry." Free leaned back into the stone corner of his cell and looked in the lieutenant's eyes. "And I am thankful for what you did back there. But I'm innocent. My troubles with Jubal go back to Fort Brown at the end of the war . . ."

When Free had finished detailing his difficulty at the Boca Chica retreat, he could see a genuine look of concern and anger appear on the lieutenant's face.

"Sergeant, we are short manned here at the Fort. The soldiers spend a good portion of their time in the field trailing hostiles, coming in only as needed for recuperation. As much as it pains me, I'm detailed to carry a supply line to Fort Richardson and the Jacksboro settlement this morning. And that's an order I can't ignore. But I will do my best to get you some help."

Free knelt and began to scribble in the dirt. "I understand, Lieutenant." He drew a circle and then stretched another line in a southwest direction. "I figure Mr. Goodnight is heading southwest around Fort Concho." He pointed to the line's end. "We're here." He placed his finger on the circle. "How far do you figure the drive herd is from us?"

"I would imagine that to be eighty or ninety miles. About the same distance as to Jacksboro. Why?"

"Other than you, Lieutenant, I know of only two other men who would help me. One is here," he pointed to the end of his drawn line."

"I hate to say it. But we have no riders going south, Sergeant. And I would be derelict in my duty to send a single rider toward Fort Concho. An army uniform riding alone in that country would invite every Comanche within a hundred miles to take his scalp. And I certainly can't send a force of men."

Frustrated, Free slapped his hand across the dirt drawing. "My only other hope would be from an old war friend, Parks Scott. And I don't have any idea where he might be."

"Does he deal in mustang horses?"

"Yes." Free felt his heartbeat race at the lieutenant's question. "Do you know of him?"

"Better than that, I know where he is."

Chapter 15

The Comancheria, Texas 1868

P arks Scott set his eyes on the rolling dust cloud
  expanding across the West Texas horizon.
  With out hesitation, he took spurs to the mustang beneath him. He had left Jacksboro at the first
show of daylight, riding straight into the heart of
the Comanche range. Parks whipped the reins hard
across Horse's shoulders, urging him farther into
the Comancheria. He knew a lone rider in Indian
Territory was on a hard course, but word from the
Fort Griffin supply line was that an ex-slave, Free
Anderson, sat in The Flats jail awaiting hanging.

Summoned by Judge Freemont, the only
preacher within a hundred miles of the Fort was
making his way to attend the hanging. Even on
foot, he carried a three-day jump on Parks. If the
preacher reached The Flats before him, his old
friend would be swinging from the hangman's
noose by nightfall. Parks reckoned the best chance
of saving both their hides lay in the reddish cloud
ahead. The storm might force the preacher to seek
shelter and keep the Comanche and Kiowa to their
camps on the Clear Fork.

Pulling his bandana up over his nose, Parks
slapped the mustang's flank and ran headlong
toward the approaching dust.

Thousands upon thousands of stinging specks
blasted Parks' face. No matter which way he turned

or ducked his head, the flying sand continued to pelt him. It seemed as if all the topsoil in West Texas was screaming across the Comancheria molded into a storm by howling, unrelenting winds. The horizon had merged sky and land together, painting a solid canvas of orange, undetectable as to up or down. Parks knew to stop on an open prairie during such a storm was to invite death, but he had to cover Horse's eyes and nostrils.

He pulled reins on the pony and tied both leather leads to his left wrist. In the blinding storm, he would have no chance of survival if he lost contact with Horse. He dismounted and pushed his head tight against his saddle. Even with his head pressed hard into the leather, the swirling winds forced his eyes shut. He edged his right hand down Horse's flank, searching for his saddlebag. Stretched away from the protection of his shirt, his bare wrist felt the incessant bite of stinging sand as he rummaged for the saddlebag clasp. Frantic, he worked his hand in a circular motion until he touched metal. He pushed the flap up and pulled a woolen shirt from inside.

Moving cautiously, he worked his way forward along Horse's neck, holding a death grip on the reins. Unable to open his eyes, even for a second, he searched in desperation for the mustang's nostrils. The shirt beat against his face unmercifully as he tried to swing it onto Horse's face. Gripping both sleeves, he moved away from Horse and swung the shirt over the pony's nose. As the wind continued to beat the shirt against Horse's head, he tied the two shirtsleeves together under the pony's jaw. The shirt extended slightly to the front of the animal, resembling a woman's bonnet. If he kept Horse straight into the wind, he figured the shirt would work as a deflector. If not, the sand would fill Horse's lungs, literally drowning him on dry land.

He placed his shoulder under Horse's head and pulled down on the excess shirt hanging below the mustang's nose. Holding tight, he reached for his knife and cut out a long slender piece of cloth. He wrapped the shirt just below Horse's forelock and extended the excess material around the side of the animal's eyes. He prayed that the shirt would hold, knowing neither of them would survive the storm if it didn't.

Feeling his way back toward the saddle, he remounted and spurred the mustang into the wind. "Easy, Horse." He spoke, fully aware his words would never reach the mustang's ears. Traveling with the velocity of the sand, they blew harmlessly to the east.

Parks pulled a tight rein on the mustang and tied his hands to the saddle horn. Using the wind as his compass, he moved Horse forward, hoping he could stay on trail. The strength of the wind kept his chin pushed deep into his chest. He prayed the storm would die soon.

Wandering and adrift on the prairie for what seemed hours, Parks could feel the sand penetrate his nostrils. Loosening his hands, he reached for his bandana and realized only shreds remained of the thin cotton cloth. He knew the stories of riders found with their lungs completely full of sand and figured he would have to set Horse down, when suddenly, the mustang pitched and took a strong stride toward what Parks reckoned to be south. His legs felt the mustang shudder, take off at a gallop, and stop almost immediately. The sudden jerk snapped Parks' chin upward. Deaf, his ears filled with sand, Parks opened his eyes and looked at his surroundings. They were free of the blowing storm and standing in a shallow bed on what had to be the Clear Fork of the Brazos.

Parks rolled out of his saddle and fell facedown in one of several shallow pools of water. After several seconds of holding his face in the stream, he threw his head backward and exhaled a loud breath. "Horse, you did it! I'd kiss you if you weren't so ugly!"

He watched the mustang toss his head up and down trying to dislodge the shirt covering his face.

"Hold on," Parks stood and untied both shirt pieces from the pony. He took the larger of the pieces, dipped it into the water, and cleaned the sand from Horse's eyes. "Get yourself a drink," He rubbed the mustang's nose. "Now we just need to figure out where we are."

Chapter 16

The Flats, Texas 1868

The midday June sun beat down on Free's prison. Rock and iron absorbed the sweltering heat and radiated it inward like a cook stove. *Where are you, Parks?* He anguished. Reaching for the water, he tilted the bucket toward his mouth. He took a long pull, swishing the water in his mouth before swallowing. Warmed by the sun, the tepid water was barely drinkable. But if he wanted to survive, he knew he must keep his body filled with the liquid. Three days had passed since his sentencing and Lieutenant Swafford's departure. He reckoned that even on foot, the preacher would arrive within a day.

He knew as soon as the preacher walked into The Flats, Jubal would hang him. "Think, Free!" he yelled aloud. "Quit feeling sorry for yourself and think!" He realized being a freedman was not an easy lot. In fact, he reckoned living free was much harder than trying to be free. Now sitting alone in a cell, he realized waiting to act would not keep the law's rope from his neck. All of his free life he had abided the law. But Jubal's law offered backroom justice served up by bad men who held little regard for right or wrong. He held his arm out and looked at his blackness. "How can one color cause so much difficulty in a man's life?" He spoke aloud, wondering how future generations of freedmen would fare in turn. Deep in thought, he swore, *I survived Anderson Farm and the great war by fighting everyday, and I'll be danged if I let Jubal Thompson take my life now without a fight.*

At mid-afternoon, the heat of the day sapped the life from even the strongest body. Most of the town, including the sheriff, expended little energy during this time. It was siesta, as the Mexicans called it. Man and beast stayed under whatever shade presented itself, bringing The Flats to a standstill. Clara used the siesta as an opportunity to sneak food to him. As she approached the jail side of the street, she lifted her apron slightly and ran for the alley where he was confined.

Free smiled as she knelt beside the cell and produced a folded cloth from her apron.

"Free, I managed to save some biscuits and honey from this morning's breakfast," she smiled.

Even cold from the morning meal, the biscuits still carried a pleasing smell. "Clara, I owe you so much. I know you have risked your life helping me out this past week."

He saw her eyes sparkle at his words.

"Free, I believe you would have done the same if it was me inside this cell."

Free reached through the bars and touched her arm. The skin was smooth and cool, even under the noon heat. "Well I promise to make it up to you when this is all behind me."

"I'll hold you to that, Free."

He took a great breath through his nostrils. Her smell was fresh, like prairie flowers after a rain. He dipped the biscuit in the honey-laden cloth and popped it into his mouth. "Oh my." He relished each bite. The sweet amber coated his throat as he swallowed. "How can such a small biscuit," he looked at the unfolded cloth sitting on Clara's lap, "taste like heaven?"

He could feel her happiness in watching him as he eagerly swallowed the remaining biscuits.

"Mmmmm," he growled. He closed his eyes to enjoy the remaining sweetness left in his mouth.

"And now for the best part," she said.

He opened his eyes in surprise. "What? What else?"

From inside her apron pocket, she produced a small tin cup with a cloth tied around the top. He could smell the aroma immediately. "You didn't?" He moved as close as possible to the bars breathing in the unmistakable aroma of black coffee.

After savoring the pungent black drink, he lay back on the dirt floor of his cell and stared out to the noon sky. "Isn't it funny, Clara," his eyes focused on the building clouds above, "that such small pleasures are what truly make us happy?" He rose up suddenly. "What about you, Clara? How did you come here? Tell me about you."

He could see a look of surprise cross her face. Caught off guard, she appeared unable to speak.

"No one's ever asked me anything about myself before."

"Com'on." He gestured a finger toward her. "I need to know about the girl I'm falling in love with."

"Free!" She turned her head. "You don't even know me!"

She could not hide her smile, and he knew that her words were only an act. "I know enough, Clara." He reached for her hand. "And once this is all over, I want to see you every minute of everyday."

He watched her hand move toward his, and her shoulders fell ever so slightly forward toward the cell.

"I was born in Alabama on a farm owned by a man called Browning. As early as I can remember, I sewed for the farm. Mrs. Browning said I had a gift, that I could be a seamstress someday. And it was Mrs. Browning who taught me to read and write. When I turned fourteen, Mr. Browning sold me and my sister to a man called Mason. Mr. Mason took us on a boat to Texas and gave us his name. I slaved for him near Victoria until he ran off to the war. Mr. Jenkins bought me three years ago from Mr. Mason's wife. We stayed mostly in South Texas until a few months ago, and then he moved us here."

"But Clara, didn't you know you were free? All Texas slaves gained freedom with the announcement in Galveston on June 19, 1865. You don't have to stay with Mr. Jenkins."

"That's easy to speak of, Free, but I was fifteen, alone and held no money. I had no choice. At least Mr. Jenkins doesn't hit me and pays me every Friday for working at the hotel."

"What about your sister, Clara?" Free asked.

"I don't know. Mrs. Mason kept her on the farm. I have had no opportunity to learn of her since."

"Don't you worry; once I'm out of this mess, we'll find her."

"But, Free. How can you and I be together? I still belong to Mr. Jenkins."

"No, Clara. You're as free as I am. Back in 1863, the president said so. The congress said so. You're nobody's property anymore."

"Can it really be? Will Mr. Jenkins just let me walk off? Will people like Sheriff Thompson leave us alone? Leave us to be happy?

Free could see a look of fear steal across her face. He recognized the expression from his slave past. It was an apprehension of the unknown, the fear that your life was better as it was, no matter its harshness. A slave's fear was a powerful thing. "Look at me, Clara. I promise you that someday, you and I will go into the hotel and sit down in the dining room. And Mr. Jenkins will ask us what we want to eat? I promise that to you."

He saw her eyes smile.

"I'll hold you to that promise, Free Anderson. But what about your friend? Do you think he's coming here?"

"If he got word, he'll come. But I pray it's today, because I reckon the preacher will be here by morning." He slowly released her hand and looked up into her eyes. "I need another favor, Clara. I hate asking you, but I've got no one else to turn to right now."

"Free, you can ask anything. You are the first man who ever treated me with an ounce of kindness. You make me feel like I'm more than just a colored seamstress. What is it you need?"

"If Parks got the lieutenant's message, I can't let him ride into The Flats without warning."

"A warning?"

"Parks knew Jubal during the war also. When Jubal arrested me, he made it well known that he blamed both of us for his demotion after Palmito Ranch. If Parks rides into town and Jubal recognizes him, he'll end up in here with me. And I'm afraid we'll both hang. I need you to stop him before he rides into The Flats. He might be riding straight into a noose of his own."

Late in the day, Clara lay behind an outcropping of limestone above Panther Crossing on the Clear Fork. The rock formation gave an unobstructed view of both the riverbed and the road leading to The Flats. She scanned the valley to the east, looking for the dust of an approaching rider.

The sun still hung one hand over the western horizon, but the workday was almost finished. Mr. Jenkins would be stirring soon and wondering why her chores were undone. If he mentioned that to the sheriff as he took his dinner, Jubal might come looking for her. "Come on, Mr. Parks." She pleaded, continuing to scan the landscape.

From the far end of the riverbed, a lone object appeared, shimmering in the heat. In an effort to block the sun, she half closed her eyes, cupping them with her hands as the object began to take form. It was a man on horseback riding to beat the devil toward The Flats.

Hurrying around the far side of the rock formation, she scooped up her skirt to run. Her feet twisted sideways on the loose rock causing her to simultaneously run and slide down the steep incline. She couldn't believe how fast the mustang was galloping along the sandy riverbed.

At the bottom of the hill, she began a desperate dash to the river, waving her hands and screaming wildly, only to see the rider just go by her. She screamed as loud as she could to the man's back. "Mr. Parks! Stop Mr. Parks!"

Out of breath, she continued running and yelling after the speeding pony, only to turn her ankle on a flat river rock and land face first in the shallow water.

"No!" She pushed her body from the river. "No!"

Downstream, she saw Parks had reined in the mustang and turn. He was heading back to her at a slow trot.

Exhaling in relief, she stood in the middle of the Brazos and smoothed her dress, trying to look presentable.

"Ma'm," Parks asked while removing his hat. "Do I know you?"

"Mr. Parks?" she stammered. "Are you Mr. Parks Scott?"

"Yes ma'm, I am. And if I might?"

Clara realized she had not introduced herself. "My name is Clara Mason. I am a friend of Free."

"Are you OK, Miss Mason? That must have been quite a tumble you took."

"I'm fine, Mr. Parks, and please, call me Clara. I'm so glad I caught you before you rode into town."

Parks replaced his hat and stepped down from his horse. He let the reins drop and lightly tapped his horse's flank. "Go on, Horse."

She turned toward the riverbank. "We best sit and talk."

After explaining the situation in town, Clara waited for Parks to speak. The slender cowboy looked at the sky and the soon-to-set sun.

"It appears Free has walked off into a hornet's nest. I've worried for two years that Jubal would try to take his revenge. He's a man not to trifle with."

Clara could see a tension building in Parks' face. His brow had furrowed, and his nostrils flared with each breath. "What can we do, Mr. Parks?"

GET
4 FREE BOOKS!

You can have the best Westerns delivered to your door for less than what you'd pay in a bookstore or online. Sign up for one of our book clubs today, and we'll send you **4 FREE* BOOKS**, worth $23.96, just for trying it out...with **no obligation to buy, ever!**

Authors include classic writers such as
LOUIS L'AMOUR, MAX BRAND, ZANE GREY
and more; PLUS new authors such as
COTTON SMITH, TIM CHAMPLIN, JOHNNY D. BOGGS
and others.

As a book club member you also receive the following special benefits:
- **30% OFF** all orders through our website & telecenter!
- **Exclusive access** to special discounts!
- **Convenient** home delivery and 10 days to return any books you don't want to keep.

There is no minimum number of books to buy,
and you may cancel membership at any time.
See back to sign up!

*Please include $2.00 for shipping and handling.

YES!

Sign me up for the Leisure Western Book Club and send my FOUR FREE BOOKS! If I choose to stay in the club, I will pay only $14.00* each month, a savings of $9.96!

NAME: _____

ADDRESS: _____

_____

TELEPHONE: _____

E-MAIL: _____

☐ **I WANT TO PAY BY CREDIT CARD.**

☐ VISA   ☐ MasterCard   ☐ DISCOVER

ACCOUNT #: _____

EXPIRATION DATE: _____

SIGNATURE: _____

Send this card along with $2.00 shipping & handling to:

**Leisure Western Book Club
1 Mechanic Street
Norwalk, CT 06850-3431**

Or fax (must include credit card information!) to: 610.995.9274. You can also sign up online at www.dorchesterpub.com.

*Plus $2.00 for shipping. Offer open to residents of the U.S. and Canada only. Canadian residents please call 1.800.481.9191 for pricing information. If under 18, a parent or guardian must sign. Terms, prices and conditions subject to change. Subscription subject to acceptance. Dorchester Publishing reserves the right to reject any order or cancel any subscription.

JOIN NOW!

"Clara, is there any way we can get Free's horse rigged and ready to ride?"

"I suppose. Samuel at the livery might help us if I had coin to pay him."

"I've got coin. Don't worry about that."

In a moment's time, Clara saw Parks' face relax, his eyes fixed in total concentration. It was as if he knew the outcome of tonight's showdown. "What are we going to do with Free's horse?"

She saw his eyes brighten.

"You're going to tie it in front of the sheriff's office. Once you've got him tied, you get back to the hotel. You go about your chores just like any other day."

"Mr. Jenkins is going to be plenty mad at me, Mr. Parks. How am I going to explain why my chores are not finished? How am I going to explain where I've been all day?

"You tell Mr. Jenkins that the sheriff has had you busy all afternoon. You tell him that, and let me take care of the rest."

"But what are you going to do, Mr. Parks?" She saw a stern look come over Parks' face.

"I don't have it all worked out, Clara." Parks stared west toward The Flats. "All I do know, is I've got a hanging to stop."

Chapter 17

The Flats, Texas 1868

Against a purple sky, the late afternoon sun cast off a multi-colored fan, in a brilliant display of orange and red, the last remants of daylight reached skyward. Bolstered by the cooling night air, The Flats would soon be brimming with activity.

Parks had followed the Clear Fork in a wide arc around the town, preferring to enter from the west below Fort Griffin, offering only a silhouette to any curious onlooker. With Clara behind him, he entered town at a slow gait, his hat pulled low over his eyes.

The livery stable was the first structure off the main thoroughfare and a hundred yards from the hotel and saloons. From Clara, he knew the sheriff ate dinner at the Jenkins House every evening near dark. After his meal, he would walk next door to Kelley's for whiskey. If Parks was going to rescue Free, he needed the sheriff to keep to his nightly routine. He glanced at the sky and figured they had half an hour to wait.

Turning onto the main street, he could see the open doors of the stable. A large rectangular corral sat next to the building and held several horses and mules.

"That tall one, that's Free's horse. He calls him Comida," Clara whispered in his ear.

Parks eyeballed the animal and then shot one last gaze down the main street. He wanted to make sure they had attracted no attention during their entrance. As all seemed well, he pulled the reins right and walked Horse into the livery.

Inside, Parks dismounted and helped Clara down. He took a quick inventory of the stable. He looked into the offices and saw a slender individual in a livery apron coming out to greet them.

"Need to put your horse up?" the man asked. And then seeing Clara, he said, "Hi Clara. Friend of yours?"

"It's Samuel. Right?" Parks interrupted.

"Yes," the man replied. "Do I know you?"

"I don't need him put up, but he does need a good brushing and grain," Parks answered. "And no, you don't know me."

The livery owner turned his attention to Horse. "This animal looks like an Indian pony. You don't see many whites riding 'em around here. They look somewhat small for a full-grown man to ride. I'll have to charge you half a dollar for the brush and the grain."

Parks pulled a gold coin from his pocket and held it in front of the man's eyes. "How much for that tall plow horse outside?"

"That plugger is not for sale at the moment. He belongs to a prisoner down in the calaboose. Although he might be available in a couple of days."

"Why a couple of days?" Parks asked.

"That prisoner, a colored fella name of Anderson, is set to hang as soon as the Jacksboro preacher arrives."

Parks drew another gold piece from his pocket.

"If he's going to hang, why wait? That horse looks dragged out to me. You ought to sell him while you have a buyer."

Standing beside him, Parks watched Clara nod her head yes to the livery owner.

"Well, I guess I could go ahead and sell him, but if the sheriff finds out, there will be the heck to pay. I'm gonna need another gold coin if I'm going to risk his anger."

"I tell you what, Samuel. You throw in that Spanish saddle and blanket hanging over there, and we've got a deal."

"Then we've got a deal, Mister. I don't much cotton to the sheriff's ways no how."

Parks smiled and dropped three gold coins into Samuel's palm. "Now, Samuel, if you'll take care of my horse, I'll get that plugger from outside."

A half hour later, brushed and fed, Horse stood in contentment as Parks cinched the saddle around Comida. Handing the reins to Clara, he said. "You know what to do. Just make sure you go back to the hotel after you tie him up. You'll be safe. It appears that the entire town is either in the hotel or the saloons."

"Mr. Parks, I—,"

"Shhhh." He stopped her and placed his hand on her shoulder. "It's OK. Everything is going to work out." He helped her up in the saddle and watched as she rode out of the livery. As she disappeared from his view, he turned and walked into the livery office.

"Here's your receipt, Mister. What name do you want on it?"

"You know what, Samuel?" Parks smiled. "Don't worry about that receipt."

"But you need a receipt to prove ownership."

Parks tapped two fingers against the butt of his holstered Colt and replied. "I know the owner, Samuel. He's sitting two hundred yards away in jail right now."

"You aiming to give that colored fellow back his horse?"

Parks studied the livery owner. "I aim to free him from jail, Samuel. He's been set-up in a foul way by Sheriff Thompson."

"Well, that's no surprise to anyone around here, Mister."

Parks walked forward and placed both hands on Samuel's desk. He leaned as far over the desk as possible, unsure of what he just heard. "You know my friend is innocent?" He asked in disbelief.

"Mister, you need to know right now, most folks in this town don't take favor with the sheriff. He's a bully and a chiseler."

"Then why not do something about it, Samuel? It might be you sitting in the jail next time around."

"That's easy for you to say. You go heeled and seem like a fella who can take care of himself. But Jubal is a mean sort, and he backs up his play with The Riders. I'm not looking to set my bones in the sun right now."

Parks pushed away from the desk and gazed at the man in front of him. "No, you're right, Samuel. Jubal has the perfect jig. An outlaw carrying a badge."

"And if I knowed what you wanted that colored fella's horse for, I would've given it to you. I don't cotton to bilking innocent folks. And to square things, you only owe me for the brushing and the grain."

Parks looked across the desk at Samuel, holding two of the gold coins in his outstretched hand. "Samuel, you keep the coins. If you really want to make things square, there's a favor I require of you."

The assembled clientele at Kelley's Saloon was a mixed bunch. Government surveyors, gamblers, cowboys, and dance hall girls all crowded for a spot along the fifteen feet of bar spanning the length of the building. At the west end of the bar, gamblers sat at two tables dedicated to Chuck-a-Luck and Faro. Constructed in a rush, the saloon's plank walls consisted of green wood. Within weeks of completion, the boards all warped, allowing the night air to drift through the establishment, mixing the smell of stale beer with the foul stench of buffalo tallow.

It was here that Jubal Thompson held court each night. He had a permanent table with seven chairs surrounding it placed at the east end of the bar. His chair stood against the back wall and faced the opened doors to the street. It provided him with a bird's eye view of anyone entering the saloon.

Jubal sat alone this evening, a cigar and whiskey in each hand. The crowd, loud for a weekday, but not unruly, gave him time to think. He knew his take from the rustled cattle would be plenty enough to set him up with a ranch across the border in Piedras Negras. The prospect that Free would be dead by morning brought a smile to his face. Once the colored sergeant hanged, only The Riders would need attending to, and he was more than ready for that challenge.

As he contemplated his run of good luck, he noticed Von Riggins enter the saloon. He tilted his chair back against the wall, allowing it to lean with two legs off the floor. "What's up, Von?"

"Jubal, my chores are done. Do you need me for anything else this evening?"

The sheriff tossed the remaining whiskey down his throat, wincing slightly. "You don't want to sit with me?"

"Jubal, I just want to go home and get some sleep."

"What about the sergeant?"

"Last I looked in, he was sleeping. He's locked tight as could be; I don't figure him to be going anywhere."

"He better not," Jubal chuckled. "Anyway, the Jacksboro preacher oughta show up by tomorrow morning."

"So it's OK for me to leave?" Von pleaded. "I'll be back first thing in the morning."

Jubal stared at the deputy and then waved his hand to dismiss the man. "Yeah, yeah, yeah . . . Go on Von. Just make sure you show up at daybreak tomorrow."

He watched Von turn and move quickly for the door. "Hurry, Von," he muttered, "Before I change my mind." Feeling the whiskey beginning to speak, he laughed aloud for the entire bar to hear. "Go on home and fix the missus some dinner, Von!"

As the deputy disappeared through the door, he saw Samuel Cleary gazing over the swinging doors. *This oughta be good.* Jubal had never seen Samuel inside any drinking establishment in The Flats. He studied the livery owner with amusement as the man scanned the Faro and Chuck–a–Luck tables. After a few seconds, he called across the crowded, smoke-filled room,

"Samuel, who are you looking for?" He noticed the man look his way and point his finger toward the ceiling.

"There you are, Sheriff."

"Drink?" Jubal held a half-full bottle toward the man.

"No, thank you, Sheriff. I do not partake."

"Well, what brings you down to Kelley's?" The sheriff took a long draw on his cigar, blowing the pungent smoke toward Samuel. "You don't drink. I'll bet even money you don't smoke. And God forbid you would ever want a woman." Leaning forward, half soaked, Jubal let his chair fall forward so that all four legs once again touched the floor. "So what is it?"

"Sheriff, that colored fella from the jail just came in the livery demanding his horse," Samuel answered.

"What!" Jubal sobered momentarily. "What did you say?"

"The colored fella, he wanted his horse."

Jubal snapped to his feet. The force of his action sent the chair flying back into the wall with a loud crash. The commotion brought an immediate silence to the saloon. And Jubal saw all eyes turn his way.

"What's everyone looking at!" he slurred. "Don't come in here trying to scoop me, Samuel! If you get my back up, you won't like the consequences!"

"I'm telling the God's truth, Jubal." Samuel stammered. "That colored is sitting over in your office waiting for you. I thought you might want to know, that's all."

Jubal's eyes darkened. He put his hand to his pistol and swayed toward the door. Across the street, a horse stood tied outside of the jail. Inside his office, he saw the soft glow from his oil lamp illuminating the room.

"How the—," he mumbled. Turning back to Samuel, he tossed a nervous glance. "Is he armed?"

The livery owner shook his head no.

"I'll take that as a yes, Samuel." Turning to the bar, his eyes narrowed like a rattlesnake. With a clenched jaw, he shot a hard look at the patrons. "You all heard Samuel. The ex-slave has escaped and is carrying a gun. He aims to settle a score with me." He kept a steely gaze on everyone. "Does anyone disagree?" Satisfied as to his authority, Jubal set his jaw, cast a look of hard intent toward his office and gripped the ivory handles on his Colts. *Sergeant, you can't imagine what a favor you've given me; it appears there won't be a need to hang you after all*, he thought.

Chapter 18

Across the street from Kelley's, Parks moved in the shadows of The Flats. With caution assigned to each step, he navigated the seamy backside of the town. In the darkness, the visible outline of buildings along the main thoroughfare reflected with a charcoal hue. Just past the blacksmith and Shaunissy's Saloon, he spied the lights from Kelley's and the Jenkins House. He left his stirrups in one motion and moved close to Horse's head. "Quiet, Horse," he whispered while lifting the reins over the mustang's head. Leading the pony, he crept toward the jail and his friend.

Midway to the cell, he could see the dark shadows forming the outdoor cage. "Psst . . ." he whispered toward the cage. "Psst . . . Free."

He saw the shadow of a figure rise from the cell floor and look his way.

"Parks? Is that you?" the figure spoke.

"Yeah it's me. Keep your face to the street and watch Kelley's. Let me know if anyone tries to leave."

"Clara found you. I knew you'd come."

"You sure keep trouble for company, Sergeant."

"Not at my choosing."

Parks shot a quick gaze behind to make sure he had no surprises following him. "Free, your horse is tied up in front of Jubal's office. In a few minutes, I reckon the sheriff will be heading this way to see what that horse is doing there. When he does, I aim to get his keys and get you out of here."

"Right now, any plan seems good to me."

"Just hang on and be ready."

"You needn't worry about that. I'm ready to be quit of this cell."

Parks pulled Horse's reins up close and tied them loosely around the back of the cell. "I'm leaving Horse here. And take this Colt just in case," Parks handed an ivory handled pistol through the cell door. "The chamber's full."

"Thanks, Parks. Be careful."

"I'll be back shortly." He turned, and using his hands as guides in the darkness, he followed the wall planks around the building.

From the corner of Jubal's office, he peered across the street toward Kelley's. Jubal was making his way across the boardwalk and into the street. A crowd hung in the doorway, watching. With very little motion, Parks eased the Colt from his holster and held it chest high. Even in the darkness, he could tell that the Sheriff was plenty roostered. *Big mistake, Jubal.* He thought.

He watched the sheriff walk up behind Free's horse.

"What the—!" He heard Jubal call out, apparently satisfied as to the horse's identity.

Parks could see that Jubal was stumped as to his course of action. He prayed the whiskey had blurred the sheriff's ability to think straight, and he wouldn't consider simply walking over to Free's cell. Parks knew if he did, the plan would go up the flume. "Com'on Jubal," he whispered. "Go inside your office." He watched the sheriff fix a gaze on the jail door, shake his head like a mad bull, and stagger onto the boardwalk, fumbling his Colt from its holster.

"All right, Sergeant, I'm fixing to show you a hard case!"

Parks eased around the corner as Jubal raised a boot and kicked in the jailhouse door.

"Put that gun down, Sergeant!" Jubal screamed, and the ring of gunfire filled the air.

Parks hurried through the shattered door, stopping inches from the sheriff's back. He wanted a confused Jubal to know who was behind him and whispered in a quiet voice, "Boca Chica."

"Huh—," Jubal muttered.

As the Sheriff turned toward him, Parks brought the long barrel of the Colt down on top of his head. Jubal moaned and careened back against his desk and to the floor.

"Sweet dreams, Sheriff," Parks said while reaching down to remove the cell keys from his pant loop.

Keys in hand and partially hidden by the busted door, Parks looked across to Kelley's. The onlookers had moved to the boardwalk and were walking in a tight formation toward the street. From the darkness, Parks shouted in a deep voice. "Everything's OK here! Get back to your drinking!" He kept the Colt in hand until he saw the group turn and move back to the saloon door.

As soon as the street was clear, Parks dashed for Free's cell. Rounding the corner, he heard Free shout.

"Parks! What's going on? I heard gunfire!"

"Easy, Free. That was just Jubal showing off for the crowd at Kelley's."

Parks stuck the key in the padlock and opened the cell door. "Hurry, and help me get Jubal in here."

Several minutes later, Parks leaned the sheriff against the back corner of the cell. As he turned to leave the cage, he noticed Free standing next to him, a set of shackles in his hands.

"I owe Jubal a shackle fitting," he said.

"Well hurry and lock him in because we need to be riding out pretty quick. I don't know the whereabouts of Jubal's Riders, and it doesn't seem smart to tarry too long."

"Don't worry about them. They left town the morning of my trial. I have a pretty good idea where they're headed and when they'll return."

Parks looked on grimly as Free locked the sheriff's arms and legs in the shackles.

"I wore these earlier in the week courteousy of Jubal. It only seems right to return the favor."

Untying Horse, Parks looked at his friend, "We best figure our next move."

"The way I see it, the only way to ever clear my name in this matter is to find The Riders. They'll be carrying proof of my innocence," Free explained.

"What do you know?"

"I heard them talking the first day on the trail. I was a little played out, but I'm pretty sure they spoke to having rustled cattle grazing toward New Mexico way."

"Do you have an idea of where the cattle might be put?"

Now in front of the Sheriff's office, Free stepped into Comida's stirrup. "Best I can tell it has to be around the Kiowa Arroyo. That's where they ambushed me and met up with some Kiowa braves."

Parks lifted the tobacco pouch from around his neck and tossed it toward Free. "A man deserves a chew after a fuss like tonight."

Parks watched Free cut off a plug of tobacco and poke it in his jaw.

"There's someone I need to see before we light out."

"Can't say that I blame you, Sergeant. But let me warn you, if you get seen with Clara tonight, after all of this," Parks pointed back toward the cell, "you're going to have the sheriff and Mr. Jenkins wondering as to her part. I know it's hard, but she's safer without being around us right now."

"Maybe we should take her with us."

"Sergeant, we've got a ride ahead that would drag out the most seasoned cowboy. It wouldn't be right to put Clara through that."

"I know you're right, Parks, but it sets hard in my belly leaving her like this. If anything happens—."

Parks turned Horse to the west and glanced over to Free. "Let's find The Riders; then we'll be back for Clara." With a quick kick, he set spurs to the mustang. "And after that, you can settle the score with Jubal once and for all."

Chapter 19

The Flats, Texas 1868

A voice from deep inside a well called out. The jumble of words, distant and foreign, caused a wave of confusion to build in Jubal's mind.

"Jubal!"

He tried to open his eyes, but the morning brightness caused tiny ripples of pain to tingle across the top of his head.

"Jubal! Are you OK?"

The sheriff sensed that he could avoid the pain if he kept his eyes partially closed, looking at the blur of the world through his eyelashes.

"Jubal!"

He turned toward the sound and noticed a dark figure standing above him. Gripping the bars for leverage, he tried to pull himself up, as visions of the previous night began to dance in his thoughts. He looked toward the gradual focusing figure of Von Riggins.

"Jubal! What happened? Where's the colored?"

"Von!" Jubal struggled to right himself; he could feel the rising panic in his voice. "Get me out of here!"

"Where are the keys, Jubal? Your office is busted to hell, and I can't find the keys anywhere."

Leaning against the cold steel of the cell, Jubal howled. "Get Samuel down here with some tools and bust this thing open!"

"Do you want me to find Clara and have her come over to tend your cut?"

"Just go, Von! I'm not of a mood to answer all your questions! Git!"

An hour later, after Samuel and Von took turns hammering the lock apart with a smithy sledge and chisel, the door to the cell opened.

"Get these irons off of me!" Jubal screamed. "Get them off now!" He held his arms outward as Von removed the shackles from his wrist and feet. "Son-of-a-!" He looked at Samuel, wincing with every word. He touched the wound on his forehead, feeling the caked blood. "You!" He pointed to the livery owner. "Get Clara over here now! Tell her to bring a needle and thread." He rubbed his forehead gingerly as he watched Samuel move off in a hurry and then turned to Von. "Get me some grub and coffee from the hotel, I've got to sit down for a spell and think. I'll be in my office."

Minutes later Clara stood over Jubal. "This is a deep wound, Sheriff."

"Just get me stitched up quick-like, Clara." Jubal stared at the busted door leaning against the inside wall of his office. "The sergeant had some help." He spoke aloud. "Did you notice any strangers in town last night, Clara?"

"Sheriff, please be still while I clean this wound," Clara answered. "I don't want to hurt you anymore than I have to."

He watched her soak a wool rag in whiskey.

"Jesus!" Jubal screamed as the soaked rag touched his head. "I thought you didn't want to hurt me!" He squinted, his face in pain, and he saw that Clara had jumped two feet away.

"I'm sorry, Sheriff. I didn't mean to hurt you any, but that wound has to be cleaned."

Jubal saw her fear. "It's all right; just get back over and finish up, pronto."

The pain seemed to bring his thoughts into clear focus. "Von! Is the preacher here?" he asked the deputy.

"He arrived this morning Jubal."

"Well, you put him up in the hotel, and don't let him leave."

"I don't figure he's going to want to stay now-."

"I don't care what you think, Von! You put him up at the hotel and don't let him leave. Tell him the sheriff says he is not to leave The Flats. Understood?" Jubal could feel the heat building in his neck. "We're still going to have that hanging! Only there might be more than one body for him to pray over!"

"Jesus!" Jubal hollered as Clara pulled the first loop of stitch. "You're rough as hell, Clara."

"Sorry Sheriff, I'm doing my best," Clara replied.

"Well, hurry it up will you! I've got business that needs my attention!"

Trying to throttle his anger, he spoke to Samuel, "What time did that colored come to the livery?"

"Right at dark, Jubal."

"How the hell did he get out of that cell?" Jubal wondered aloud.

"I don't know, Jubal, but he had a pistol with him. Threatened me, he did."

Jubal stared hard at the livery owner. Something

was not right, but he was stumped as to what. "Samuel, I need help in hunting down the colored and his accomplice. Ride out to the Dodge place, and tell Randolph I need to put a posse together."

"It's calving season, Jubal. I don't think Mr. Dodge is going to be receptive to letting men leave right now. What if he says no?" Samuel asked.

"You tell him I said to send some men! Tell him we're going after the men who stole his damned cattle!"

"I'm finished, Sheriff," Clara said. "That wound needed seven stitches to close."

"About time." Jubal stood and with great care placed his hat on his head. "You get on back to the hotel now." He walked behind her, and as he reached the door, he remembered a voice from the previous evening. Two words. "Boca Chica." And then he realized the identity of the sergeant's accomplice.

At mid-afternoon, Jubal stood on the boardwalk outside of his office. Even with a pounding headache and seven stitches, he was amazed at his good fortune. The two men he swore revenge on were heading straight for his Riders. He figured it didn't really matter who killed who. For when he arrived with the posse, he would take care of anyone left alive. From across the street, he saw Murph Jenkins hurrying his way.

"Here's enough grub for a week, Sheriff."

Jubal reached out and accepted a flour sack, rolled flat. "What do we have?"

"Mainly biscuits and hard tack."

Jubal tossed the sack behind the saddle of his packhorse and tied it with two rawhide straps. "Clara got you doing the deliveries today?"

"No, she's finally getting around to yesterday's chores. Now I know you have a lot on your mind, Sheriff, but if you're going to use the girl, I wish you would at least tell me so I can make my arrangements."

"What did you say?"

"Let's not get into a fuss over this, Sheriff. I'm just saying—."

"No. Tell me why Clara didn't get her chores done?"

"She said you worked her yesterday afternoon. That's why she didn't get to the hotel until after dark last evening."

Jubal glared toward the hotel. "The little—! Where is she?"

"She's over cleaning the upstairs rooms. Why? What's going on?"

Jubal brushed by the proprietor and ran across the street to the hotel. Inside, he bounded up the hotel stairs in a fury. At the top hallway, he saw Clara exiting one of the rooms. He rushed toward her.

"Hello, Sheriff. How are you feeling?"

"I should have known better than to let two ex-slaves get friendly with one another." He grabbed her by the upper arm.

"Wha—!"

"Helping a prisoner escape is a hanging offense!" He could feel her strength as she attempted to pull away. "This is thanks I get!" Releasing his grip, he swung a fist with all his force into her jaw. With no attempt to catch her fall, he watched her unconscious head bounce off the wood floor. "You made a big mistake, missy!" Reaching down, he hoisted Clara over his shoulder in one powerful motion. He could feel the anger churning in his belly as he walked down the stairway. At the bottom of the stairs, he encountered Jenkins. "Don't say a word! She's coming with me!" He pushed past the hotel owner and continued into the street.

Outside, four cowboys tied reins to the hitching post. The oldest of the bunch called out. "Mr. Dodge said you could use our help Sheriff."

"All of you, follow me." Jubal snarled and continued to walk toward his office.

As he reached the packhorse, he threw Clara's limp body over the saddle. "Tie her down! And make sure she's tied tight!"

The lead cowboy straightened Clara upright and bound her hands to the saddle horn. "What'd she do, Sheriff?"

"She pissed me off, that's what! Now, all of you raise your right hands." Putting boot to stirrup, he swung up on his horse and watched as each man lifted his hands, "Do you swear to uphold your duty as a deputy on this posse?"

He took account of each cowboy's nod. "Good." Reaching into his shirt pocket, he fished out four tarnished badges. "I pronounce you deputies for The Flats." He passed the stars to the men. "Put these on." He swung his gaze to the west. "And remember, the men we're after are sentenced to hang, but if they resist us, we'll shoot 'em where they stand."

Chapter 20

The Mescalero Escarpment, New Mexico 1868

The caliche dust of the Staked Plain spun upward in a great circular motion. Galloping hooves, pounding on the earth, broke the upper crust, causing the heavy powder to spiral like a dust devil. The air borne dust clung to horse and rider alike unfazed by the prevailing wind blowing strong from the southwest. The landscape, devoid of tree and bush, looked the same in every direction. The only visible sign of life Free could discern was an occasional prairie dog, barking from his burrow, as if to warn of danger.

Ahead, Parks kept his spurs to Horse, running the mustang at a torrid pace. They had been riding for two hours straight across the desert landscape and away from the Kiowa Arroyo. Deep inside, he knew the image of the slaughter they had found there would be hard to escape, no matter how far they ran.

Arriving at the canyon in the early morning, they found the landscape littered with buzzards. The Riders had killed the ten Kiowa braves and their horses. All of the Indians had been disfigured and left nude so they could not enter the spirit world whole. It had taken the better part of the morning to bury the braves in a mounded grave of sandstone. As they finished, Parks hung the leader's brilliant war shield on a lance to mark the site as sacred.

Life's hard enough, Free thought, *Seems a man, no matter his business, deserves some peace in death.*

After the burial, Free felt sullen and angry. Hard thoughts occupied his mind about the days ahead. There were bad men riding ahead, who left carnage behind them and who needed stopping. And Free was determined not to bury anymore of that carnage.

Riding to the farthest edge of the Llano Estacado, they reached the sheer cliffs of the Mescalero Escarpment. In front of them, rippling waves of heat rolled across the air like a raging river. The cliff walls, exposed by a million years of uplifting, exhibited gradient shades of red streaking horizontally across the entire length of the canyon. Two hundred feet below, a herd of cattle milled about lazily in the dry bed of the Rojo Grande.

Looking through field glasses, Free surveyed the scene below them. "I count five. It would be a real coincidence if that wasn't The Riders."

"I don't think there can be a doubt," Parks replied, looking around the canyon walls for any chance movement. "But we're missing one."

Free pulled back on Comida's reins and walked the horse away from the rim of the cliff. "I reckon they came into the canyon floor back to our south. If they did, I'm sure the sixth man is hidden in the cliffs there, waiting for the buyer to show."

"That would make the most sense. The walls here are too high to shoot down with any accuracy. The Riders can avoid an ambush at their present position," Parks answered.

"So the Mexicans have to enter from the south, and if they try anything funny—."

"The Riders will run the cattle on top of them." Parks shook his head in respect. "This bunch is smarter than we thought. And how they left those Kiowa in the arroyo shows they carry very little conscience."

"They're a hard bunch, that's for sure," Free rubbed his chin and looked back south. "What are you thinking right now?"

"The way I see it, we better find a position some-where above both groups, but still close enough to use the Henrys. Wherever that spot is, it's to our south. And I hope to hell we don't run into the Mexicans or the lookout trying to find it."

Free looked down into the canyon and watched the rustled cattle calmly milling about. "Parks, is there always this much fuss in a free man's life?"

Parks leaned forward in his saddle and reached for his canteen. "That seems to be the hardest part of freedom." He pulled a long drink from the blad-der. "There's always someone wants to fight you for it."

Minutes later, Parks and Free backtracked several miles to the south, staying as far off the canyon rim as possible. Here the escarpment began a gentle drop to the southeast. As the cliffs became less sheer, Parks spied a game trail falling off to his right. Winding down the perpendicularly canyon wall, the trail was narrow, no more than a foot across, but well traveled.

"Most likely big horn." Parks studied the rutted ground. "They probably use the trail to come and go out of the canyon floor." He removed the tobacco pouch from around his neck and cut a chaw. "I know that Horse can go wherever a sheep can go." He tossed the pouch to Free. "How about Comida?"

Free cut a large sliver of tobacco from the plug and

peered over the steep path. "This horse? He'll follow like a Missouri mule tailing a broken sugar sack."

Parks eased his spurs into Horse's flank, guiding the mustang cautiously down the right edge of the canyon. Loose gravel rolled under the pony's hooves as he negotiated the worn path. "Keep a tight pull, Free," he yelled over his shoulder. "And don't let your hat get over his shoulders or you'll both go head over heels to the bottom."

In the lead, Parks followed the winding trail down into the depths of the canyon. Away from the rim, the air had become stale and unmoving. Just forty yards down, the heat became stifling, causing an endless flow of sweat to leak from under his hat and onto his face.

Two hundred yards from the canyon floor, the trail cut back into the cliff, winding around a large fractured outcropping of rock. The rock splinter rose twenty feet into the air, with a palisade edge hanging toward and away from the cliff wall. As he maneuvered Horse around the formation, he felt a cool spot in the air. Parks shot a glance to his left and saw a high shadow on the cliff wall. "Whoa," he called to Horse. "Free, stop here. I think I may have found something." Anxious, Parks stepped down from his saddle as Free rode up behind him.

"What is it, Parks?"

"I hope an overhang to hide the horses," he replied. "Do you feel that drop in temperature?" Parks worked his way around the cliff side of the outcropping. Behind the formation lay an opening into the rock as tall as a man and at least ten degrees cooler than the outside air. "Bring Comida around, Free. Lady Luck may be riding with us after all."

Parks led Horse to the back wall of the opening; it was at least twenty feet deep. "It's perfect. We'll keep the horses in here, Free, out of sight from any lookouts."

"I think I need to get this saddle off Comida. He's lathered pretty good. He's game, but he's not use to the type of work we just put on him."

Parks looked at the white foam oozing from the horse. "We best get the saddles off both and let them rest. If things get too hot on the canyon floor later, we are going to need fresh legs to skedaddle out of here."

Parks uncinched his saddle and placed it on the hard rock surface of the cave. He reached into the saddlebag and removed a large wool rag. "Here." He tossed the rag toward Free. "Use this to wipe him down." Turning back to the bag, he withdrew a cotton cloth knotted at the end. Untying the cloth, he eyed the contents with a careful gaze. "I may have enough grain for two handfuls each."

"Maybe we should use only one apiece right now."

Parks nodded his head. "Let's get these horses taken care of, and then we'll see how well we've positioned ourselves."

After attending to the horses, both men walked to the overhang, rifles in hand. Looking north, the rustled cattle still sat five hundred yards up canyon. From their position, the fractured rock outcropping offered them protection from sight and rifle fire. Below, the canyon narrowed into a bottleneck.

"We're sitting pretty good." Parks searched the opposite cliffs with the glasses. "I reckon The Riders will move the cattle to this bottleneck for the exchange." He looked over to his friend; Parks could see a frown wrinkle his forehead and face. "What's troubling you?"

"Well, we've got good protection up here with the outcrop in front of us and the cave behind us, but if we start taking rifle fire, there's gonna be a lot of lead ricocheting behind us."

Parks looked around the rocks surrounding them and exhaled softly, "More of that fuss, I figure."

"I'm getting used to it." Free replied.

Parks picked up his rifle and hung the field glasses around his neck. "Let's get some rest while we can," He shuffled toward the overhang. "My gut keeps reminding me men are going to die here today."

Chapter 21

The Mescalero Escarpment, New Mexico 1868

F ree woke with a start. His eyes opened to the stark rock ceiling above him. Lying perfectly still, he listened for the noise that wakened him to repeat itself. He rolled to his right and glanced over the back of his saddle. The sound was Comida flicking his tail, trying to move a host of blowflies covering his flank. He exhaled in relief. *God some black coffee and a biscuit would taste good right now.* Pushing against the saddle, he rocked his neck back and forth in an attempt to loosen the stiffness from both the two-day ride and the leather pillow his head rested on.

Glancing over to Parks, he considered himself fortunate to have such a friend. Before rising, Free carried his thoughts to the remainder of the day and the job ahead. Though battle-tested during the war, he still felt the familiar dread of killing spread across his chest, a stinging worry squeezing his heart and making breathing impossible. He told himself to worry was nonsense, but the prospect of never seeing Clara or his mother was more frightening than anything he could ever imagine.

"What are you contemplating in such deep thought, Sergeant?" Parks lay flat on his back, his arms and legs stretched upward.

Shaken from his thoughts, Free looked over to his friend. "You're awake," he said, glad for the conversation to replace his fears.

"I feel much better, I know that. How long do you figure we've been out?"

Free shot a glance westward at the sun. "Couldn't be more than thirty minutes."

"Kind of like being in the army again. Lots of riding and little to eat or sleep."

"I can't imagine why we mustered out." Free stood and pushed his arms to the cave ceiling, trying to loosen his shoulders. "Parks, I want you to know I am most grateful, and I will always be so, for you coming to my aid. I know you have a business, and for you to leave all of that for my trouble-."

"Sergeant, you would have come in a second to help me. A man shouldn't have anything more important in his life than helping family and good friends when called on. A man with other priorities can't be much better than a varmint crawling around in the dark of night."

Free stared at the man beside him. An overwhelming sense of calm engulfed him. He knew that whatever happened today, Parks would ride drag on his trail. "Well, I owe you my life. And I aim to repay that sometime down the road."

"And I hope you're never called to that purpose."

Free nodded and looked toward the back of the cave. "Think it might be a good idea to get these horses saddled up?" he asked.

Free knew it was wise to keep his mind occupied. He couldn't afford any more doubt about the chore ahead. If he hoped to prove his innocence, then a dust-up with The Riders was inescapable this day.

"Seeing how we might need to make a quick retreat out of here, I think that's a smart play."

Free picked up his saddle and blanket and

moved toward Comida. He flipped the blanket onto the horse's back and settled it on the withers. He heaved the saddle up in one motion and laid it with great care on the animal's back. With the saddle in place, he reached under the animal and cinched the girth belt. He gazed across Comida's back, watching Parks complete the same steps. After the horses stood saddled and watered, Free reached for his Colt. He spun the cylinder, checked his cartridges, and then shoved the gun into the front of his pants. "How much ammo are you carrying?" He removed Goodnight's Henry from Comida's saddle ring and opened the lever.

"I'm carrying six in the Colt and thirty cartridges. I've got a box of .44 Henry's in the saddlebag. How about you?" Parks answered.

"I've got only what's in the Colt's cylinder and the handful of Henry shells Mr. Goodnight gave me."

"Seems we better make sure our aim is right, or we're going to have to get close with the Colts."

Free dropped the six Henry shells into his front pocket and walked toward the jagged rock palisade. The sun was hanging at eye level on the horizon, but looking down; the valley floor gave a clear view. He looked over to Parks, who had joined him. "Appears the sun won't be a problem," he said.

"No, but the way it's setting means we have to be careful that the guns won't reflect a glare to the canyon floor. They'll target us for sure if that happens."

Free saw Parks set the box of Henry shells on the rock.

"Take half."

Free reached into the box and took seven shells.

"I've got six already." He pushed the remaining shells toward his friend. "What's your plan?"

"We don't really want a problem with the Mexicans, even if they are buying rustled beeves. That's a fight for another day. We'll let them make their trade and then go after The Riders."

"If we wait until the Mexicans leave, won't that give The Riders time to head out the far side of the canyon?"

"Once the cattle are moving, we make our play on them. I figure the Mex's won't hang around to help those cowboys. They're going to drive those cattle like hell back to the border."

Free took in a deep gulp of air as the cold steel of the Henry rested heavy in his hand. The rifle issued a reminder to him that the moment was near. "And The Riders?"

"Free, just remember what they did to those ten Kiowa behind us. We open up on them; there's no way those boys will be taken alive. They'll either kill us or die trying."

Free placed a cartridge into the Henry and chambered the shell. "I know. I just needed some reminding, that's all."

"Free," Parks said, "if they want to surrender, we'll take them, but I'm not betting your life or mine on that."

Free nodded and, hidden by the rock palisade, began to move toward the far end of the outcropping three feet away. Looking to the canyon below, he saw a wall of dust rising off the floor. "Parks!" He spoke in a low whisper, "The cattle are moving." He watched Parks point the field glasses toward the opposite end of the canyon. "See anything?"

Parks balled up his right hand and flipped his fingers and thumb out twice.

Ten Mexicans. He figured, "Do you see the other Rider?"

"Yeah, he's moving along the west canyon wall at about seven o'clock. I think he's working back toward the herd."

Free looked across the canyon, but he could not pick up the man's movement with his naked eye. He noticed Parks beginning to inch his way toward the low end of the outcropping. The moment they had both waited for and dreaded was coming fast. "Parks!" he called out. "Good luck."

"Don't worry, Free; we'll get that money back," he replied.

Free peered over the rock and watched as two Riders peeled off under the cover of the herd. Each of the men moved his horse up toward the canyon wall and dismounted, using the large rocks as cover. "Did you see that? I don't think they're going to sell those cattle."

Parks rose slightly and pointed the field glasses toward the sixth Rider's location. After a minute, he slid back to the protection of the outcropping. "It's a bushwhacking, Free! They're not going to let the Mexicans leave this canyon. They aim to take the cattle and the money."

"Shouldn't we warn the Mexicans?"

"How, Free? We don't have time to get to the canyon floor from here. And if we open up, we've got three Riders unaccounted for."

Free bit his lip and looked back onto the canyon floor. "But if we start on the three we do see, we might give the Mexicans enough warning to help with the others."

"That's crazy, Free. What's to keep the Mexicans from killing us after that?"

"Trust me on this, Parks. They aren't going to kill the men who saved their lives."

"After all you've been through, I figured you to be a little more mistrusting of your fellow man. I'll follow your lead, but we've got to warn the Mexicans about that sixth Rider behind them right now. If we try the shot and miss, he won't let himself be seen again. And from his position, he'll be able to pick them off one by one."

Free looked at the sun sitting on the opposite canyon wall. "Can you blind him with the field glasses?"

Parks glanced at the sun. "It might work."

Free looked down at the Henry and squeezed tight on the stock. He knew the distance across the canyon was near the end of the rifle's range. "If you can, I'll make the shot," he said. He glimpsed toward Parks, who held the field glasses at chest level. "I know I can hit him."

"All right, Sergeant, when you see the reflection settle, that's where you shoot," Parks said. "I'm going to put the sun right in his eyes."

Free nodded and pushed the Henry tight against his shoulder, raising the metal sight on the barrel. With his left eye closed, he held aim across the canyon. A small flash of white appeared as the sun's reflection bounced from the field glasses. Without hesitation, Free squeezed the trigger.

The echo from the gun's discharge raced around the canyon walls causing all parties on the floor to freeze. Free watched as the Mexicans and Riders, startled by the shot, scanned the canyon walls looking for powder smoke. He looked to Parks and saw his friend had the field glasses trained on the opposite side of the canyon.

"That's one Rider who won't leave here today," Parks called.

Free rose and placed the Henry's sight on the lead Rider, who was searching the canyon walls in desperation, trying to locate the shooter. "Drop those guns, Johnny!" he screamed. His echo bounced around the canyon walls. "Or I'll shoot you like a dog!"

He could see the recognition on Johnny's face, but Free stared in disbelief as the Rider calmly holstered his pistol and reached for his rifle. *Is he crazy?* Remembering Parks' warning, Free chambered another shell, just as Johnny's rifle reached his shoulder. In a slowed-down world, the Henry belched fire, and the lead Rider flew from his saddle. Free kept a hard look as Johnny clutched his chest and then, in disbelief, pulled his hands away, watching the spreading crimson staining his shirt and hands. The .44 slug had found its target.

As his surroundings sped up once more, Free felt his body pulled downward. Glancing toward the ground, he saw Parks, sitting, his hand gripping a fold of his shirt.

"You offering them a target, Sergeant?"

As if awakened, Free could see the rock chips flying from the wall behind them. The deafening roar of gunfire echoed below, and thick smoke covered the canyon floor. It seemed flying lead filled the whole escarpment.

"We need to move down to the south end," he heard Parks yell over the gunfire. "Away from the ricochets."

Free nodded his head and followed Parks on

hands and knees the twenty or so yards down the outcropping.

Taking a deep breath, Free rose and peered over the rock cover. Below, he watched as the Mexicans moved forward on two Riders beside the now still-body of Johnny, the belch of gunfire accompanying them. Outgunned, the two fell beneath a hail of Mexican lead. Scouring the canyon floor, Free spotted one of the bushwhackers still hidden behind a large boulder. His back to Free, the man held aim on the lead Mexican. Free levered the Henry and in quick succession threw two shots down on the man. The slugs bit into the sandstone boulder near the Rider's head, spitting rock chips in the man's face. Surprised, the Rider turned and scanned the canyon walls for the shooter. Working the lever once more, Free sent a bullet into the man's chest, kicking him back against the boulder. Even at his distance, Free could see the look of shock on the man's face as he slid slowly down the rock facing. Glancing once more around the escarpment, Free watched the ten Mexicans descend on the last Rider, who was hidden behind an outcropping on the far side of the canyon. Guns roaring, the Mexicans fired without stop, causing the man's body to jerk like a puppet as each bullet found its mark.

And then silence. With the firing stopped, Free surveyed the canyon floor. The cattle, behind The Riders when the bullets started flying, had turned and were stampeding toward the north end of the canyon.

At the far end of the canyon, he saw ten men on horseback adorned in traditional Mexican wide brim hats. The vaqueros, with ropes spinning, rode directly for the herd.

"What the . . . ?" Free muttered.

Parks rose and looked down on the canyon. "It appears the Mexican's weren't so trusting in their dealings with The Riders."

Free had never witnessed the skills the Mexican cowboys possessed. The first vaquero, riding a buckskin mustang, ran headlong for the lead steer. Using his horse as leverage, he turned the steer right. The next vaquero in line used his pony in the same way and herded the next group of steers to the right. This was repeated by all ten vaqueros in succession. Within minutes, the entire stampede was turning in a tight circle and headed back south toward the bottleneck.

Looking down, Free saw one of the Mexicans ride from the canyon floor toward the palisade wall. He nudged Parks with his elbow and pointed down to the Mexican rider now looking in their direction.

"*Hola*!" The man yelled out. "*Gracias amigos*! Now please show yourselves, so we don't have to come up and kill you!"

Free looked over to Parks and watched as the lieutenant removed his bandana from around his neck. "What are you doing?"

Tying the bandana to his rifle barrel, Parks pushed the gun skyward over the rock barrier and yelled to the Mexican below. "I'm coming out! *Yo camarada*!"

"Parks!" Free yelled. "This was my idea; if it goes bad, I'm the one who needs to deal with the consequences!"

"Can't let you, Sergeant. You have Clara and a mother to worry about, and you're a much better shot with that rifle. We've come this far for that bag of money, and I'm going down to get it. You keep the Henry trained on the hombre doing the hollering. If anything looks odd, you shoot him in the chest. No matter what else happens, you make sure you shoot him first."

Free nodded his head, "Make sure you give me a clear shot at him, Parks."

"Oh don't worry, Free, I'll make sure there's plenty of air for a bullet between him and me."

"What are you going to say to them?"

"Right off, I'm going to make sure that lead Mexican comprendes that the gun which shot that Rider off the canyon wall is aimed at his heart."

Chapter 22

"Y ou are only one hombre."

"No, there are more," Parks answered matter of factly. He made note the Mexican carried two pistols, turned butt out, in the waist of his pants. "I reckoned they would have better aim at your heart from up there."

The Mexican gazed up toward the cliffs. "Yes. You are a tricky one, maybe?"

"No," Parks replied, looking past the man to the activity behind him. The other Mexicans were methodically dragging the five Riders shot during the gunfight into a line. He watched them lay each dead Rider on his back, arms placed across his chest. Parks looked back to the lead Mexican, "Just a man who wants to leave here alive."

"But you are my friend. No? Did you not shoot at the bushwhackers? These bad men who wished to kill me and my amigos?"

"Something like that." Parks put the rifle's butt on the dirt, removing his bandana in the process. "Did you know these cattle were stolen?"

"Stolen cattle? How could I know such a thing? I am a business man."

"Well, they were stolen and these men," Parks gestured toward the dead Riders' bodies, "placed blame of the thievery on my partner." He turned and pointed back up the cliff wall. "The man with the gun aimed at your heart."

"Jefe!" Parks heard one of the Mexicans call out. He stepped to his left and saw the man holding up the head of one of the Riders by a handful of hair.

"This one is still breathing!"

The lead Mexican walked over to the Rider and lightly slapped his face.

"Señor? Señor? You have done a very bad thing. You ask to sell us cattle, and now we find out from our friend that you have stolen these cattle. If there were any trees in this God-forbidden desert, I swear I would hang you. *Dios mío.* But instead, we will cut your throat."

Parks heard the Rider moan and watched the Mexican draw a long knife from his belt. "Wait! He called out with a steady voice. "Let's finish our business first!"

"What business, *señor*?"

Parks put a scowl to his face. "Our business of the stolen cattle and clearing my partner's name."

The Mexican shrugged and walked back toward him. "OK. We finish our business, and then I kill him."

Parks held a steely gaze on the lead Mexican now facing him. "What can we do to let everyone leave here happy?"

"But hombre, I have the cattle, and I still have the money. I am already very happy."

Parks stepped close to the man and whispered under his breath.

"Speak louder, hombre. I did not hear you."

Parks waited for the man to step closer. With lightning like speed, he yanked his Colt and set the barrel in the Mexican's belly. Smiling, he grabbed the man's waistband, pulling him close and whispered. "How happy are you now?"

He watched the Mexican's face drain in color.

"I thought you were my friend."

"Oh we're friends, just not close friends." Parks leaned in closer. "Now, here's what I need for you to - ."

"You are Texas cavalry?" The Mexican interrupted.

"What?" Parks asked, somewhat confused by the Mexican's rapid pointing to his hat.

"Texas cavalry. You have the pin in your *sombrero*. Texas cavalry. Colonel Rip Ford?"

Parks furrowed his brow. "You know Colonel Ford?"

"*Si*. Colonel Ford is *el Jefe Grande*. I alone helped Colonel Ford keep the Brownsville port open for Mexico during the great American war. We let the colonel know when the damned Yankees come. And in return he keeps the port open for my family."

Parks saw the opportunity to further his cause with a small lie. "Colonel Ford is my uncle."

"No! This is good. Colonel Ford is my friend, and you are Colonel Ford's family."

"So we are friends?"

In a series of quick motions, the man moved his hand back and forth between the two of them. "Oh yes, hombre, friends."

Parks holstered the Colt and held out his hand. "My name is Parks. And don't forget there's still a rifle on your heart, friend."

A broad grin came across the Mexican's face. "You are a very careful man, hombre."

"I find I tend to live longer that way."

"Yes. Yes. That is the way. Come amigo, now you meet my friends."

Parks followed the man as he moved toward the nine other Mexicans.

"*Muchachos*! Look! The nephew of Colonel Ford! He is the one who save us from the ambush."

Parks glared at the men, who were busy rifling the corpses of the Riders. On hearing the name of Rip Ford, they all stood and greeted him with up-lifted arms and smiling faces. He returned the smiles but kept one hand near his Colt as the lead Mexican turned back to him. "I need the money for these cattle." Parks kept his gaze on the man's face, never looking down or giving a blink.

"Oh! So you want to steal the money?"

"Not steal." He gave a tight-lipped smile. "You have the cattle; I need the money to pay the ranchers back for their losses."

"Maybe we only give half?"

"No. You give me all the money, and we leave as friends." Parks stepped close to the man. And I tell my uncle Rip Ford that - ," Parks pointed to the Mexican.

"Juan de La Pena."

"That, Juan de La Pena is owed many favors from our family." He saw a big smile form on the Mexican's face.

"*Bueno*. Yes. As a token of our friendship and in honor of your uncle, I give you the money for the ranchers."

Juan whistled toward the Mexicans, now busy removing boots from the corpses. He spoke a few words in Spanish, and one of the men rushed to a pack mule tied behind Juan's mustang. The man untied a saddle pack from the mule and carried the bag to Parks, dropping it at his feet.

"*Gracias, Señor.* I will never forget your bravery and courteousy." Parks reached over to pick up the pack. "And I hope you will never forget the rifle that is still aimed at your heart."

"Still so careful! This is OK. Remember me to Colonel Rip Ford, *por favor.*"

"I will do so." Parks bowed.

As he turned and walked away, he heard Juan call to his men. "¡*Andale pronto muchachos!* ¡*Vamanos por la Mexico!*"

Parks turned and saw the ten vaqueros from the north end of the canyon begin to position themselves to move the cattle out of the canyon. The nine men with Juan stepped to their horses, and showing off, they sank their spurs while pulling the ponies up on their hind legs.

Looking to Juan, he watched the man mount his steed. Behind him, tethered by ten feet of lariat, the wounded Rider lay on the ground. "Juan!" He called out. "What about him?" He pointed to the Rider.

"Oh, no worry. I am going to drag him to safety!"

Parks heard the laughter of the Mexicans ring the canyon floor. He looked up at a grinning Juan and then down to the Rider. "Señor de La Pena!" He shouted, holding up his hand. "Before you go! *Necesito un favor más!*"

Through his rifle sight, Free watched the Mexicans begin their departure from the canyon floor. Twirling lariats, loud whoops, and cries accompanied their exodus as they drove the stolen cattle toward the south.

Danger passed, he lowered the Henry and leaned it against the rock outcropping. Looking through the field glasses, he observed Parks in an animated discussion with the lead Mexican. The Mexican sat atop his horse, gesturing wildly at the wounded Rider tied to his saddle horn. He watched Parks reach into a saddle pack and reveal what appeared to be a stack of money. "What are you doing, Lieutenant?" he wondered aloud. He kept his focus on the Mexican now dismounting his steed. Parks was pointing to the Rider with one hand and waving the money around with the other. He saw the Mexican shrug his shoulders and flip his hand toward the Rider as if granting permission. Almost immediately, he watched Parks kneel beside the Rider and observed conversation between the two. After several minutes, Parks stood and re-opened the pack. He watched his friend withdraw the money stack once more and hand it to the Mexican. That done, Parks turned from the Rider and started a slow walk back toward the game trail. Free could see anguish scribed on his face.

Setting the field glasses on the outcropping, he hurried down the trail. Then suddenly, the canyon echoed with the sound of a lone gunshot. The gunfire caused Free to jump in surprise. He threw a quick gaze to where the shot seemed to come from. On the canyon floor, he saw the lead Mexican standing over the unmoving Rider while pushing a pistol into his waistband.

With little thought, Free began a mad run toward Parks, wanting to make sure his friend was safe. Slipping and sliding as he maneuvered the snake-like pathway, he kicked small rocks and dust up in his wake. As the trail emptied onto the canyon floor, he came face to face with Parks.

"Parks! Are you OK?"

"I reckon so."

"What went on down there?" Free reached out for Park's rifle offering to loosen his load. "What were you and the Rider talking about? What'd you find out?"

"Let's sit a minute, and I'll tell you."

Free stepped off the trail and found a slick area of rock sloping toward the canyon floor. "This OK?" He sat down on the warm stone.

"I took some of the money for the stolen beeves and paid that lead Mexican two hundred U.S. to give that wounded Rider a quick death."

Free inched closer to his friend. "You did what had to be done, Parks. Don't blame yourself for what was due him someday."

"I know, Free. I told the man he had two choices, tell me what I needed to know and be shot mercifully or play it hard and let the Mex's drag him to Mexico. He knew he was gone up the flume. Still, leaving a man helpless, even a bad man, and then having him shot like a dog twists my gut into knots."

Free put his hand on Parks' shoulder and squeezed tightly. "My father once told me that a man is required to pay for past wrongs." Free glanced out to the Riders' bodies littering the canyon floor. "And while the method of that payment may seem harsh, very rarely is it unjust."

"Sounds about right. Your father seems to have been wise to the world."

"I believe he was." Free looked back to Parks. "It looks like you got the money for the cattle." He nodded toward the saddle pack. "That's probably gonna give Jubal more reason to be on the shoot for us."

"I believe our friend Jubal is heading for us right now. If he was able to deputize a posse yesterday, he's only a two-day ride from here."

"With The Riders away, how could he raise a posse? The Flats doesn't seem to have the sort of folks willing to give up their days hunting for rustlers."

"His best play would be to tell the big ranchers he needed men to hunt down the escaped prisoner who stole their cattle."

"Sounds like Jubal's playing a dangerous game."

"According to that Rider, they would steal cattle at night as rustlers and then go looking for the thieves during the day as the law. It was a convenient way to move the cattle. If they were come upon, Jubal could claim they had recovered the herd. Left alone, they would slowly move the herd out near New Mexico, waiting for their Mexican buyers."

"Where do you figure that leaves us?"

"Well we got two things on our side. We've got the sheriff's money, and we've got two days to figure where we want this thing to end."

Free stood up and dusted the seat of his pants. "You know this thing can only end one way, Parks." He grabbed the lieutenant's hand and pulled him to his feet.

"I've known that since the day I rode into The Flats, Free." Parks stared solemnly at his friend.

Free set his back teeth together and clinched his jaw. "Then you know," he set a hard gaze to the east, "that I'm the only one who can end this thing with Jubal."

Chapter 23

The Comancheria, Texas 1868

A quarter-moon hung high over the dark western sky, while on the eastern horizon, a reddish glow began its daily ritual. The southwest wind, energized by the rising orange globe, gust steadily, offering a cooling breeze to offset the approaching desert heat. Holding little idea of where Jubal and his posse might be, Free and Parks pressed their horses across the New Mexico border and back into Texas.

Crossing out of The Staked Plain, Free saw Parks pull reins and bring Horse to a halt. "What's up?" Free lifted Comida's reins and stopped beside Parks.

"I reckon we might want to come in from the north this time around. I think we best figure Jubal's following the Salt Fork toward the arroyo."

Free reached down for his water and took a pull. "You thinking about confronting him before the arroyo?"

"It might give us the bulge. If we wait on the flat land above the arroyo canyon, the posse will spot us right away. And I sure don't want to wait inside the funnel like cotton for picking. The river bends north for a ways before it runs south again. And the northernmost bends hold plenty of high bank."

"What about cover?"

"Cedars litter that stretch of river. Our only worry will be avoiding the Kiowa and the Comanche. Both groups run the north bank in that part of the county."

"Sounds like more fuss." Free pointed to the tobacco pouch hanging around Parks' neck.

"Appears so."

"Well we've made it this far." Free caught the tossed pouch with both hands. "No sense in being cautious now." He cut an end off the tobacco and placed it into his cheek. "That would be the smart play."

Swinging north, the two men began a hard run, galloping the horses at full speed while deftly avoiding the dangling limbs of cedars lining the upper stretch of the Salt Fork. The river snaked through the landscape creating natural sand bars beyond each bend. At a small rise just before the river headed south, a flat overhang covered a large portion of sand bar. Free watched Comida lift his head into the wind, the smell of the river in his nostrils.

"Up ahead," Parks yelled out. The lieutenant pulled his reins and slowed Horse to a trot.

The ride out of New Mexico had eased the tension of the day, and feeling flush, Free took his spurs to Comida's flank. As he slapped the reins, a blur of earth rushed toward his face. The red soil of the upper Brazos filled his eyes with stinging ferocity. Blinded, he pulled hard on the reins, without response. Beneath him, he could feel Comida pulling away from his body. His shoulder dug hard into the ground and the sensation of rolling repeatedly whirled in his head. Spinning out of control, he spied Comida sliding behind him. The horse's eyes opened wide with confusion. *Everything's so slow*, he thought. Then blackness covered his vision.

* * *

"Get up!"

Free felt his shirt pulled up into his armpits, his body dragged backwards by an unknown force. Instinctively, he dug his heels into the ground trying to stop the movement, but to little avail. The events seemed to be moving in double quick time.

"Free! Don't fight me!" he heard a voice screaming.

Looking up, he could see Parks' face above him. Confusion spun in his head, paralyzing his thoughts.

"Com'on, Free. Push against the ground!"

Free tried sitting up, but he was moving too fast to keep steady. He looked back to Parks and saw panic in his face. Uncertain as to his course, he began to kick at the ground like a mad bull. Within seconds, the sky turned green, alive with the swoosh of cedar branches whipping over him.

"What's happened?" he finally found his voice. "What's going on Parks?"

"Kiowa! They shot Comida from under you!"

Free felt all movement stop as Parks released his shirt. He rolled onto his belly and looked back toward the prairie.

"Can you fire a gun?" Parks asked.

Fumbling toward his waistband, he dug around his pants but came up empty handed. "I must have lost my pistol when I went down. And my rifle's on Comida." Fifty yards to his front, he saw Comida lying on his side. Two arrows pointed skyward from his neck, his head still.

"Comida," he muttered. And then his military training came back. He took a quick accounting of their position and observed they lay hidden in a circle of cedars.

"We've got the overhang protecting our rear," Parks called out as he sorted ammo on the ground in front of them. "You take the Henry. And I'll keep the pistol."

"OK." Free shook his head as he began to grab .44 shells.

"We don't have much ammo, Free, so if there's more than fifteen or twenty out there, we may be fixing to go through the mill."

"Fuss," Free muttered. "Just more fuss."

Ten minutes later, Free noticed the prairie grass alive with movement. He wiped the sweat from his eyes and tried to focus on the area by Comida's lifeless body. "Parks, I may be imagining things, but it sure looks like the ground is moving out there."

Parks set the field glasses to his eyes. "Nope, your eyes are fine, Free. There is a whole passel of Kiowa crawling on their bellies toward us."

"How many is that?"

"A bunch more than we have ammo for. Take a look."

Free took the glasses and saw the steady movement of the Kiowa toward the overhang. "Sure looks like a raiding party, the way they're painted up."

"Appears they aim to take scalps, that's for certain."

Free kept his gaze through the field glasses and watched as one of the braves moved to the backside of Comida. The Indian swung his left arm over the saddle with bow in hand, while his right hand remained hidden. Free could see what appeared to be the tip of an arrow strung in the bow. "They're getting ready to check our range."

"Damn!" Parks cursed.

Free saw the first arrow fly. The flint tip arced gracefully in the air and then descended, landing twenty feet in front of their position. The arrow point embedded deep into the earth.

"Haw!" Free screamed out. Hoping his bravado might push the anxiety from his body. He set his eyes back to the glasses and removed them just as quickly. "Can't be!" He pushed the glasses to Parks. "Take a look."

"At what?"

"Look at that Kiowa rolled up behind Comida. Look at his right arm and tell me what you see."

Parks trained the glasses on the dead horse. "That looks like the war shield we placed on the graves in the arroyo."

"I thought so too." Free continued to watch the Kiowa leader, observing him use hand signals to move his braves forward. "They're out for revenge!"

"It would be nice if they had an idea we gave their dead braves a proper burial."

"Maybe one of us should go out and tell them." Free removed the glasses from his eyes and rolled over to face Parks.

"That's a mighty big risk, Free. There's no telling what kind of reception those Indians might hold for either of us. And they sure don't seem to be anxious for a powwow right now."

"Well, I reckon it's die in here among the cedars or die out in the open prairie. I'm game for either, but I prefer the open." He looked out to the prairie while untying his bandana. "And for the first time in my life, not being white might give me a little edge."

"I reckon you're right, Sergeant. If we can communicate to the chief that we buried his own, it might defuse this situation. But unless you speak Kiowa, you best let me go. I learned a little of the language from my daddy."

"I can't let you do that, Lieutenant. It's high time that I started carrying some of the load here. I'm going out there."

"Well, if you're determined to go, give me the Henry and keep a shot open between you and the chief. If things go bad, I'll shoot him first. It will buy us a little time."

Free pushed the rifle toward Parks and picked up the Colt. Rolling on his back, he slid the pistol into his waistband. "Wish me luck."

In a slow and deliberate manner, Free stepped from the cover of the cedars. He had tied the blue bandana to a rawhide strap on his hat, hoping to make the cloth readily visible to the Indians. As he exited into the open prairie, he began a series of rapid arm movements, waving the hat back and forth across his body.

He saw the Kiowa braves, one by one, begin to appear from the knee-high prairie grasses. As each stood, he could hear their shrill war cry. A series of yips that was devastating to a man's courage. Hoping they understood some English, he began to yell. "Friend! I wish to talk! I am a friend!" From a few yards to his right, a brave charged, bow in hand. Free continued his frantic waving. "Friend! Friend!" The savage, on a mad run, strung an arrow and prepared to shoot. Figuring he was done in for sure, Free dropped his hat and grabbed for the Colt. He swung the pistol from his waistband and held it head high on the advancing Kiowa brave, ready to cut loose.

Chapter 24

The Comancheria, Texas 1868

Parks watched as the Kiowas set on Free. Seeing the Sergeant had his Colt on the closest brave, he swung his rifle toward a grouping of braves to the left. He readied his finger on the trigger, about to pull, when the rushing Kiowas abruptly stopped and commenced with a series of rhythmic chants that filled the whole of the prairie.

"Aungaupi! Aungaupi Ch`i!"

Parks glared as Free lowered the Colt and stood perfectly still. The raiding party now began a slow procession toward him, their weapons pointed downward. Parks listened intently to the individual chants of the braves as they encircled Free.

"Aungaupi Ch`i!"

With a sense of relief, Parks watched Free drop his hat and pistol, holding both hands palm up. He rose from his position in the cedars in amazement, watching the first brave rub Free's head.

"Aungaupi Ch`i," The brave sang.

Within seconds, all of the Kiowa had closed ranks on Free. Each seemed intent on rubbing his head and touching his clothing.

"What's going on?" Free hollered to Parks.

From the stand of cedars, Parks called out. "Just be still, and we might leave here with our scalps. They say you're the buffalo man."

"Hā chò."

Parks walked with authority toward the Kiowa

braves, knowing the Kiowa did not tolerate fear, especially in their enemies. The Indians sat with crossed legs in a circle around Free. He could see the confusion set on his friend's face. "It's OK," he whispered to Free while approaching the Kiowa chief. He showed respect, holding his hands away from his body, palms up. Offering no threat, his holster hung empty on his hip.

"*Hā chò,*" the chief replied.

Parks stopped several feet short of the band, watching as the warrior with the war shield stood. Like many of the Kiowa, the chief was tall, standing well over six feet. Parks took a close look at the painting and feathers on the war shield. It was indeed the same one from the arroyo.

Parks shot a glance at Free. "The buffalo is a very sacred animal to the Kiowa. And they think your hair is that of a buffalo. You are a very strong sign to them, part buffalo and part man. It's the only reason we're alive right now."

Parks took his focus back to the chief. "Do you speak English?"

"I know some of the white man's tongue from the time before the Medicine Lodge Treaty."

"And I speak some *Kai-gwu.*"

"How is it a white man can speak the *Kai-gwu* tongue?"

"It was taught to me by my father. He was a Texas Ranger, who fought the Kiowa north near the Red River. He spoke of what great warriors the Principal People were."

"*Àho.* You hold the tongue well, Son-of-a-Ranger. I am Tsen-tainte."

"I am Parks."

From the corner of his mouth, Parks spoke to

Free. "He is known as White Horse. I've heard of him; he's big medicine. After Medicine Lodge, he cast his braves with the war faction of the Kiowa." His gaze still set on the chief, Parks made a circle around his heart with his right hand, then formed a cross inside the sphere. "Tsen-tainte, you are well known to us. We only wish to pass through the Kiowa land. We mean no harm to any Kiowa."

"But the whites have already done great harm to the Kiowa. The whites trick my brother, T`on-syan. The whites promise repeating rifles to hold cattle at the Buffalo jump. And then the whites kill the Kiowa brothers."

Parks clenched his jawbone as White Horse shook the war shield violently. "Tsen-tainte, *Aungaupi Ch`i*, and I came after the murder of your brother. We . . . ," Parks used one finger to gesture toward Free and then back to himself; "gave T'on-syan and his braves a proper burial." He pointed his hand skyward holding his wrist. "So the crow and vulture would leave their bones in peace. We placed the war shield of T`on-syan on the burial mound to show this was a sacred spot."

"*Àho.*"

Parks observed White Horse make a series of hand signals. When he finished, the raiding party all rose and marched toward the Clear Fork.

"What did he say?" Free asked as two of the Kiowa braves walked behind them.

"They're going to take council with the wind, and after that he'll let us know our fate. And these two," he motioned to the braves at their backs, "are to make sure we wait around for White Horse's verdict."

* * *

Parks sat on the bank of the Salt Fork next to Free. Below them, he viewed the Indians kneeling in the sandy riverbed, singing and chanting. The Kiowa had built a small fire on top of several flat rocks from the riverbed. As the fire burned down, White Horse placed dampened prairie grass on the coals. The wet grass caused the fire to issue a white smoke.

From the cedars behind them, Parks heard the tree branches rustle in the wind. Brushing against each other, they created a drum-like rhythm. As the smoke climbed from the riverbed, the gusty wind sweeping in from the prairie shaped the smoke into a dancing figure. The white plume flattened, drifted west, and then rose in a column before drifting back to the east.

"Do you still have the pistol?" Parks whispered while staring at the rising smoke.

"In my waistband, under my shirt."

"Well, after their council, if White Horse makes any motion with two fingers across his eyes, be ready to let that Colt fly."

"What do the two fingers mean?"

"It means the wind has told them we are not friends of the Kiowa. And the Kiowa always kill their enemies."

"I could open up on the two behind us. You could mount Horse and be a long way from here. You know no Indian pony can catch him."

"As much as I don't want to die out here today, I can't imagine living with the knowledge I ran out on a friend."

"But you don't even have a gun?"

Parks looked down at the Colt in Free's waist. "I'll manage. If things go bad, just make sure you count six Kiowa coup starting with these two." He nodded his head backwards.

After twenty minutes of observing the wind, Parks watched White Horse pick up two handfuls of river sand and cast it into the coals, extinguishing the fire.

"Looks like they're finished," he whispered to Free.

"What's the chance we're going to survive with our hair?"

"It all depends on how he read the smoke."

The chief and his party walked up the bank from the river below. As they approached, Parks stood, noticing Free's hand resting on the Colt's handle through his shirt.

"The wind has given us a great sign. *Aungaupi Ch`i* is a brother to the wind." The chief swung his arm in a wide arc from his right to his left. "From the west to the east, he will lead the *Aungaupi* against the whites. And the Kiowa will sing his song for many years to come. The wind has spoken. You are free to ride this land."

"*Āho.*" Parks nodded. "But Tsen-tainte, the Kiowa have by accident killed *Aungaupi Ch'i's tséeyñ*. And now he is afoot."

"This is true." White Horse responded. "*Aungaupi Ch`i* is free to choose any *tséeyñ* from our string. The pony *Aungaupi Ch'i* chooses will be marked with his medicine sign. This will tell all Kiowa he is a sacred being who rides the Principal People's lands unharmed."

Free walked a tight circle around the Indian pony he had chosen from the Kiowa string. The animal, high in the withers and long boned below the knee, was a magnificent brute. He was captivated watching the Indians prepare the mustang for marking. One of the Kiowa braves held the pony's upper lip between his teeth while another brave punched a hole through the mustang's ear with a slender piece of bone. The pony remained calm throughout the procedure.

"Pinching the lip keeps them from jumping around," Parks remarked.

Free moved close to the pony's head and watched as White Horse removed a decorative string of hair from a pouch around his neck. The Kiowa Chief pushed the hair pipe through the pony's ear and looped it around itself. Using a woven piece of hair from the mustang's tail, he fixed the ornament in place. This was the medicine sign that allowed him safe passage through Kiowa land.

With the pony marked, White Horse stepped back, slapped his chest three times, and with a catlike vault, mounted his horse. Uttering a series of yips, the chief called his party to leave. Heading north, and without looking back, Free heard him sing.

"Your choice in ponies is good, Aungaupi Ch`i.
The Kiowa must leave you now,
but we await your medicine.
Till that day, stay strong."

"That was mighty quick." Free watched the departing Kiowa disappear into the prairie.

"When the Kiowa are ready to move on, they go quickly. I've heard tales that a Kiowa band can break their camp and move in as few as twenty minutes. Appears they have no concept of small talk." Parks studied Free's new pony. "I hope you prize what you've just gained."

"What's that?" Free threw Comida's saddle blanket over his new mustang.

"You became a friend of the Kiowa and by association a friend of the Comanche. You've traveled a long road, Sergeant. To arrive at this place, at this time, is a fine accomplishment."

Free tossed the saddle over the pony's back and cinched the girth under the horse's belly. "Well, if I'm not able to show my innocence soon, the only road I'll be traveling is the road to a hanging."

"The time for that is nearly on us," Parks held out Free's retrieved Colt and Henry. "I figure we'll see some sign of Jubal and his posse no later than tomorrow, maybe this afternoon."

Finished with the saddle, Free placed the bridle and bit to the pony and taking hold of the Colt, slid the pistol into his waistband. "I reckon we best get ready then," he slipped the Henry into his saddle ring. "I can't see Jubal riding all this way just to arrest the two of us."

"What he can't know is we've already put a spoke through his wheel."

"How's that?" Free held the pony's reins in hand and led the horse toward the cedars above the river.

"He has to be thinking he can box us in from the east, while his Riders trap us from the west." Parks walked Horse into the first line of cedars and tied him to a large branch, the animal's hindquarters exposed to the prairie behind them.

"How is he going to explain the saddle pack of money we're going to offer the posse?"

"Think about it, Free. He'll kill anyone he needs

to, just so he can continue his lawless scheme. I reckon that posse will never leave this prairie alive, and we'll be left to carry the blame."

Free wrapped his reins around an overhanging limb and secured the pony next to Horse. "Then we better make them see what side of the law Jubal is riding on."

"I suspect the locals don't care much for the sheriff or his Riders. I'm hoping the posse doesn't either. Given the opportunity, I think we can show them the real Jubal Thompson."

Free let his gaze wander to the east, down the Clear Fork. "You figure he's going to ride right down the riverbed?"

"He's too cautious for that. They'll probably stay on high ground trying to avoid any ambush. Most likely, he'll ride down the north bank since it has the higher elevation."

"He'll be riding straight to us."

"I'm counting on it. It's the smart play."

Free moved from the cedars and faced Parks. "Let me guess; we're going to hide in the prairie grass and let him ride up to our horses, tied up in plain view."

"If we're going to get the opportunity to state our case, we best get the bulge on the posse."

Free gazed out to the prairie grasses bending in the breeze and glanced back to the lieutenant. "Well, it certainly worked for White Horse and his bunch."

"And we have one other worry."

Free looked into Parks' eyes. "What else?"

"That southeast wind that's been digging into us all morning looks to be building moisture from the gulf."

Free took a quick look skyward. "Rain?"

"Not just rain. With the temperature rising and the north sky turning green, I figure we're due some thunder boomers by late in the afternoon."

Free paused and then gestured toward Parks' tobacco pouch. "More of that fuss, I reckon."

Chapter 25

The Comancheria, Texas 1868

The rain fell in deafening sheets of gray. Overhead, Free listened to the menacing rumblings of thunder growling fair warning of each impending bolt of lightning. As far as he could see, great streaks of electricity danced crosswise in the sky before plummeting to earth with tremendous concussion, leaving the burnt stench of sulphur in its backwash. With every crack, his body stiffened tightly, maddened by nature's assault.

Sitting under a great expanse of cedar limb, he kept a steady gaze to the northeast. At his back, the nearly dry riverbed had become a swirling current raging from bank to bank. He set the field glasses on the ground, as it had become impossible to see through them in the downpour. "You think Jubal will stop on account of the rain?" he yelled over the loudness, spitting water with each word.

"There's nowhere to stop on the prairie. They have to keep moving toward the north bank where they might find cedar cover!"

Free watched a waterfall of rain leap from his hat brim and puddle between his legs. "How long do these storms last?"

"Depends on the wind! I reckon this one will blow by us quick now. There's some blue showing in the north!"

Free wiped at the continuous stream of water running from his face, then looked back to the east. "Hopefully real quick!" He nudged Parks, while pointing to the wide turn of the Salt Fork where it began its long jaunt north. "There are riders coming!"

"Can you tell how many?"

"I count six!"

"We best work our way into the grass; they'll be on the overhang soon!"

Free rose and peered from the cedars. A gradual slope from the overhang would hide the posse's view momentarily. He felt Parks' hand slap his back.

"Let's go!"

Free ran, slightly hunched over, to a spot thirty yards in front of the stand of cedars and dropped to his belly. Almost on cue, the rain slowed to a drizzle.

He looked over to Parks lying on his belly, his head turned toward the northeast. From out of the now falling mist, the first rider's horse appeared, walking at a slow gait. The rider, wearing his slicker, leaned forward over the saddle, his head lowered toward his chest. One by one, in single file, the posse crested the incline to the level ground of the overhang.

Free flattened his body hard into the rain-soaked ground. His head, raised only inches above the prairie, surveyed the approaching riders.

With the hard rain ceased, the lead rider lifted his chin and looked about the overhang. With a slow pull on his reins, he stopped his mount and signaled to the left. Free could see he was pointing to the horses tied in the cedars. The posse all dismounted with care, their heads on swivels studying the surrounding landscape. From the back of the line, a short figure moved with caution toward the horses, gathering in the reins of all six.

"That's got to be Jubal," Free whispered. He watched the sheriff point to different locations along the stand of cedar. Four of the posse members nodded at his directions and moved apart, walking in measured steps toward the interior of the cedar thicket, each lifting a Colt from under his slicker as he went. Jubal held the remaining rider by the neck and eased back toward the incline, the horses in tow.

"What do you make of that?" Free watched the two move behind the horses and out of view from the trees.

"I don't know, but we best move now. Those cowboys will be coming out of the trees shortly, knowing something's cockeyed. I'll head for the cedars, and you come up behind the other two."

Free nodded and began backtracking in the grass, keeping himself between the posse's horses and Jubal's vision. He crawled toward the incline, moving down the hill to position himself directly behind the sheriff. As he began inching forward toward the two figures, he heard Parks shout, "Put down those Colts! Or fear for your life!"

With a burst of energy, Free rose from the ground and with cat-like quickness crossed the distance between himself and the sheriff. With a fixed purpose, he pushed his Colt into the back of the shorter man. "Don't move a muscle, Jubal, I've got you dead in my sights!"

Free kept a hard gaze on the two as the sheriff, still holding the rider by the neck, turned, his pistol pressed hard against the cowboy's temple.

"You best drop that Colt, Sergeant, or your girlfriend here gets one in the head."

Chapter 26

The Comancheria, Texas 1868

T he sight of Clara gagged with a pistol to her head stopped Free dead in his tracks. Shocked, he dropped his gun hand slightly away from its target. In that instant, Jubal, a wide smirk crossing his face, plucked the Colt from his grip.

"Is that your best play, Sergeant?"

Free looked down to his empty hand, the realization of the moment jolting his senses. He looked up, casting a steel gaze into Jubal's face.

"You harm her, and I swear you'll pay!"

"I don't think you're in any position to be barking out threats, Sergeant."

Free cast a quick glance to Clara. Her eyes, opened wide, carried an unrestrained look of fear. Furious, he swung his gaze back to see Jubal call over his shoulder.

"You best drop your weapon too, Lieutenant! Or your friends are both up the flume!"

Staring past the sheriff, he blurted out. "Do as he says Parks! He's got the drop on me, and he's holding Clara!"

Within seconds, Parks walked toward him, hands pushed to the sky. Free knew they were soon to pay the consequence for underestimating the sheriff's cunning.

"Get them all handcuffed! And tie their feet! I

don't aim to let anyone bushwhack me this go!" Jubal screamed.

Handcuffed, bound, and forgotten for the while, Free glanced down to Clara. She had worked the gag out, and her lips mouthed, *I'm sorry.* Waiting until Jubal turned away, Free whispered, "Don't worry. I'm going to get you out of here." Looking to the posse, he watched Jubal glance back and forth among the four men. Out of hearing distance, he nevertheless could tell the sheriff was worked up about something. After much pointing and stomping, the cowboys nodded, mounted their horses, and left the overhang, riding to the west. "Where do you reckon those fellas are headed?" Free asked, watching the cowboys take spurs to their horses.

"More than likely, they're going to look for stolen cattle," Parks answered.

As the cowboys disappeared past the horizon, Free looked to Parks. "He knows the cattle are gone. Why would he send them off?"

"I figure he wants to question us without anyone listening in."

The posse gone, Jubal hurried over to the ponies tied in the cedars and rustled through each mustang's saddle pack. Not finding what he was looking for, he untied the bedrolls, tossed each on the muddy ground and knelt beside them. After patting down every inch of cloth, Jubal swept the bedding aside and cursed in anger.

Free grinned, guessing the sheriff's frustration might begin to work in their favor. "Looking for your money, Sheriff?"

"Be careful," Parks uttered.

The sheriff gained his feet and rushed toward them, cursing as he came. Setting his jaw, Free prepared himself to withstand Jubal's wrath.

"Where is it?" the sheriff screamed.

With cool composure, Free glanced down as Jubal grabbed his shirt, lifting him slightly off the ground. Unfazed, he raised his eyes and stared square into the sheriff's face. "You want the money? You're going to do it my way," he said in a dark tone.

Jubal let go of his shirt, allowing him to fall back to the ground and sending a stab of pain through his backbone. Wincing, he nevertheless spoke with clear authority. "Don't threaten Clara again, Sheriff, or you'll never see the money."

"I'll—," Jubal raised his hand in a striking position.

"You can't scare us anymore, Jubal. You're going to kill us all no matter what. So why should I die and give you the money?" Free watched the sheriff clench his jaw, knowing he had him thinking.

"I'll let the girl go."

"That's right. She goes free, right now."

"Not before I get the money!"

"It's not going to happen that way, Jubal. She goes; then I tell you where the money is."

"How do I know you'll keep your end of the deal?"

"Because I want her alive more than I don't want you to have the money. She leaves right now on my pony." He nodded toward the Indian mustang.

Free held his breath as he and the sheriff stared hard at one another. He knew his ploy would work only if he showed no tell in his expression. After several minutes, he heard Jubal screech a string of curse words, then walk over to Clara.

"I'll hunt her down again if you back out on me!"

Free looked over to Clara as Jubal cut the ropes around her feet. "Clara, you get on my horse, and you ride away. Don't go back to The Flats. You head north, you hear?"

"But what about you and Mr. Parks? I can't leave you here like this."

"You just go while you can, Clara. You take my mustang and don't stop until you're far, far away. Go north!" He saw tears well in her eyes and run down her cheeks.

"Com'on!" he heard Jubal scream.

Fighting against the handcuffs in anger, he watched helplessly as Jubal grabbed Clara's arm and pulled her toward his mustang. A grimace set on her face as she climbed into the saddle. "Just go, Clara. Head north."

Exhausted on the inside, he kept his jaw taut, only satisfied after she disappeared into the distance of the Comancheria.

A stinging pop shook him away from Clara.

"Where's the money, Sergeant?"

Free felt the sting of a welt rising on his cheek. "How did you know we had the money?"

"Truth be told, I didn't know which of you would come out of this alive. But since you and your friend here were riding back east, I had to figure you disposed of The Riders and were coming back to clear your name. You needed the money to do that, Sergeant."

"And you didn't mind if your men died in the process?"

"They were cattle thieves. How was I supposed to know? Now, I know Clara is away, but if you don't start talking about where my money is, I aim to begin working on your friend, and you won't like watching what I do."

"Look back to your north." Free tossed his head toward the prairie. There's a dead horse out there. Shot by Indians. Look under his neck and you'll find a saddle pack. Your money's in there."

Free felt Jubal's open hand softly pat his cheek.

"I knew you'd learn to respect me, Sergeant."

Seething, Free watched the sheriff traverse the prairie toward the body of Comida.

"You know he's going to drag us back to The Flats and hang us as quickly as he can," Parks said.

"Just fuss," Free replied. All his concentration, now was focused north into the Comancheria.

Chapter 27

The Comancheria, Texas 1868

With the rain stopped, the West Texas sun made its presence felt once more, saturating the air with a dripping heat. The hotness energized the prairie to life. A loud, frenzied hum filled the air, now swarming with hordes of mosquito and black gnats. The pests, looking to feed on or aggravate any willing prey, seemed particularly attracted to human sweat. Free shook his head wildly from side to side, trying to find some relief from the incessant blackness filling his eyes and ears. In the foreground, he could make out a blur of Jubal packing his horse with the rancher's money.

"Little buggers are heck after a rain, aren't they?" The Sheriff grinned.

"What happens now?" Free spoke with tight lips, trying to keep the bugs out of his mouth.

"I've got one more chore; then I'm hauling you and your partner back to The Flats. The preacher you requested is waiting for you there." Turning back to the horses, Jubal removed Parks' Henry from the saddle ring and dropped the rifle into a leather holder hanging from his own saddle. With ease, he stepped up in the stirrup and plopped onto his horse. "You boys stay comfortable while I'm gone."

Free watched Jubal turn his horse west and ride

in the direction of the posse. Looking to Parks, he asked. "What's he up to?"

"I don't know, and I can't think with all these bugs feeding off me. You may think I've gone loco, but follow my lead." Parks rolled over on his side and began rubbing his face and ears in the muddy ground. When he rose up, he had a thin layer of mud covering his neck, cheeks, and ears. "It'll keep them off you."

Free nodded and rolled to his side, battering his face in the mud. As he regained an upright position, he looked backed to Parks, staring at his friend for an instant then said, "I promise to get us both out of this mess."

Two hours later, the sun began a slow descent over the Comancheria. Free sat miserable. Thirsty and tired, he found that his arms had developed numbness from being locked behind his back for so long. Still, he had no idea where Jubal was or when he would return. As the last vestige of light hung in the sky, a lone gunshot echoed from the west. The reverberation lasting over five seconds indicated the shot was some distance away.

"There's no doubt that was my Henry," Parks stated.

After some duration, three more gunshots rang out back—-to-back. Then quiet once more.

"You don't think?" Free looked west. A worried frown settled on his face.

"It was his last obstacle," Parks replied. "Now nobody can dispute his word."

"How could-." Free shook his head, unable to finish while trying to make sense of such savagery and evil.

"Now he can tell everyone we did it, and no one can say otherwise."

Free struggled once more against the handcuffs, as much in anger as fear. Crazed, he screamed with all of his energy at the sky. Exhausted, he closed his eyes in an effort to regroup his feelings. He pictured his mother in Missouri and Clara riding a wild mustang into the Comancheria. Opening his eyes, he glanced over to Parks. "Sorry about that outburst."

"More fuss, I suspect," Parks responded.

Later, Jubal rode back onto the overhang, with one of the cowboy's horses in tow. The day's light, almost exhausted, hid all but an outline of the sheriff.

"You boys doing OK?"

"We heard gunfire." Free watched Jubal dismount and lead the cowboy's horse toward the cedars. "What happened?"

"A tragedy." Jubal replied.

With dread as to the sheriff's pronouncement, Free looked on as Jubal tied the animal next to Horse, then turned back toward him and Parks.

"I still don't know how you two disarmed that cowboy. But thank God, I was able to get the drop on you both before you killed me too."

"You think all of your killing was really worth the money?" Parks asked.

"Killing sworn deputies of a posse is a hangable offense, Lieutenant. Helping the colored escape would have only landed you some jail time, but now, you've really stepped off in it."

Free stared in disbelief. "How'd you get so far away from the rest of us, Jubal?" He watched the sheriff pick up his canteen and cross to him.

"Much as I can't stand killers, I'm going to give you both some water. I aim to make sure you're in good condition for the ride into The Flats tomorrow."

Free accepted the few precious drops of water eagerly, savoring the liquid as it ran down his throat. He watched Parks accept his ration, then observed the sheriff untie his bedroll and toss it on the ground several feet away. Removing the saddle from his horse, he set it at one end of his bedding, then brushed his horse on the flank. The animal flicked its tail and, moving away from the over-hang, walked toward the prairie grasses.

Later, sitting alone in the night, Free could feel his mouth salivate as the pangs of hunger rumbled in his belly. Even in the dark, the distinct scent of flour and dried beef assaulted his senses. He swore in silence as he listened to Jubal chew the food with an open mouth. Free figured he wanted to make sure his bounty was known. Then from the blackness, he heard.

"You boys best get some sleep; you've got a long ride to The Flats tomorrow."

Chapter 28

The Comancheria, Texas 1868

Clara held a tenacious grip on the galloping mustang's reins. The brutish pony had been running at full speed for almost two hours. Not accustomed to riding so far, so fast, she bobbed up and down with each stride of the animal, jarring her lower back and creating a stabbing pain that traveled the length of her spine. Her inner legs squeezed hard into the pony's sides in an attempt to control the bouncing.

Physically exhausted, she needed to stop. All of her muscles, constricted tight by the combination of fear and suspense, screamed for relief. Pulling the reins had no effect on the mustang, who continued his run with fixed determination. Her strength failing, she wrapped the reins around the saddle horn and gripped the pommel with both hands. The evening sky, cleansed after the rains, blended into a pallet of red, orange, and purple, reminding her of the lateness of the day.

She knew she had to get help. Free and Parks would hang if she didn't, but she was uncertain as to who might aid her. Free had told her not return to The Flats. And she knew he was right, for as much as the town folk might despise the sheriff, they would never stand up to him for an ex-slave. She lowered her head, trying to focus on Free's last instruction to "go north." He had repeated the phrase several times, so it had to be important, but each bounce against the saddle carried her concentration from his words back to the beast beneath her.

As darkness pushed the last portion of daylight below the horizon, the pony rolled his head left, lifting his nose into the wind. With several loud snorts, the horse shortened his stride and shook his head as if agitated. Rising up in the saddle, she felt the mustang slowing. Exhaling in relief, she relaxed her vise-like hold on the saddle horn. In that instant, the pony lurched to a complete stop, and Clara felt her body moving forward, across the mustang's head at an incredible speed. She watched the ground rushing to meet her; then a deafening thud echoed in her head, and all around her went dark.

A gnat buzzed in Clara's ear. Irritated, she tried to slap at the pest but could not find the strength to lift her arm. Flickering streaks of red flashed across the back of her eyelids. She felt herself smile, content to watch the strange dance. On instinct, her body tried to rise from the cool prairie grasses, but a heavy weight pressed against her chest keeping her down. With great effort, she opened her eyes and found herself staring into the face of an Indian. Black paint streaked his nose, and a great set of feathers adorned his head.

"Aungaupi Ma!"

Clara could hear the Indian chanting over her. Confused, she remembered the mustang throwing her off his back. She rolled her eyes, looking behind for Free's horse, and she saw a circle of savages all staring at her, pointing and chanting.

"Aungaupi Ma!"

She looked back toward the Indian hovering

over her. He removed his hand from her chest and pulled her from the prairie floor. Regaining her balance, she rubbed at a bloody scrape stinging her forehead. Still woozy, Clara realized night had set on the prairie and without thinking, she walked toward a fire burning several feet away. As she sat staring into the flames, the direness of the situation took shape in her mind. She had heard many stories about the torment Indians issued to women captives. She glanced around the camp at her captors, wondering as to her fate and wishing she had stayed with Free.

The Indian wearing the headdress strode toward her, pointing with great animation at Free's mustang, now tied to a string of ponies.

Not knowing how to proceed, she pointed to her chest and then back to the horse. "It belongs to a friend." She spoke in a loud voice, hoping the volume might make her words understandable to the Indians. "He sent me to find you," she said, the realization of Free's instruction now clear to her.

"You know the Buffalo Man?"

"You speak English?" Clara felt tears well in her eyes, as the anxiety of the past three days released its hold over her body. "You speak English!" She sobbed, her shoulders bobbing up and down in concert with her crying. "You speak English!"

"Where is *Aungaupi Ch`i*?" the Indian asked.

Clara could see that his face held no concern for her situation or her tears. "*Aungaupi Ch`i*?"

"The Buffalo Man."

She felt the Indian rub her head.

"Like you," he continued. "*Aungapui Ma*."

Realizing the meaning, she laughed between sobs and stared into the sun-hardened face of the

Indian. "He needs your help! He sent me to find you!" she exclaimed.

"Where? The Kiowa will go to help *"Aungapui Ch`i."*

"On the north bank of the Salt Fork."

The Indian looked back to the south, then motioned to one of the others. Within minutes, a brave stood in front of her offering her a stringy, reddish meat and a bladder of water. Famished, she accepted the bounty and ate the food without hesitation.

"I am called Tsen-tainte. Chief of the Kiowa."

Clara bowed her head and asked. "When can we go to the Buffalo Man?"

"Soon." he replied. He dropped to the ground beside her. "First, you must tell everything."

After talking for what seemed like hours, Clara glanced over to the Kiowa chief. He removed his gaze from the dancing flames in the fire pit and taking a knife from his waist sash began to scratch a map in the dirt. After several of the braves looked at the dirt drawing, he rubbed his hand over the picture, removing the image from the ground. Standing, he pointed to a spot in the sky several arm lengths away from the rising moon.

"Yi P'hay!" he spoke aloud.

Unsure of what was said, she watched the chief extend his left arm toward the sky, palm up and push his right hand over the open palm.

"When the moon moves two hands in the sky," he said, "We go."

Chapter 29

North Bank of the Salt Fork, Texas 1868

F ree squinted as the mid-morning sun beat down on his brow with a blinding intensity. His hands, bound to the saddle horn, prevented him from bending the brim of his hat to shade his eyes. Jubal had tied him and Parks to their horses before leaving the overhang earlier in the morning.

Now, a half-day ride from The Flats, they both faced the looming prospect of a hangman's noose. He knew they had almost run out their string. Glancing over, he noticed Parks scanning the land on both sides of the river.

"Looking for anything in particular?"

"The cavalry. It's funny that all my life, Colonel Ford has been there when I needed him, and I figured he might make an appearance here today."

"We're not in the bone orchard yet, Lieutenant. You and I have been through the mill before. We're going to come out of this just fine."

Trailing behind, he heard Jubal call out.

"You boys shut your big bazoos. I'm trying to figure where I'm gonna spend this money, and all your jabbering is distracting."

"It's not too late to do the right thing, Jubal," Parks hollered out.

"He's right, Sheriff," Free joined in. "You can still hand the money back to the ranchers. The court will take favor with you for doing that kind of thing."

"I'm gonna miss both you boys. And when I get to Mexico, I'll toss a whiskey in your memory."

Free looked at Parks and shook his head. Since New Mexico, he had tried to understand Jubal's side of their dustup. If he were in Jubal's shoes, he might have the same grudge against a soldier who cost him a corporal's rank. And during war, things happen that cost men their lives. So, regardless of Jubal's actions at Boca Chica, Free could empathize with the decisions he made. But this wasn't wartime, and he could not abide needless deaths because of a man's greed. Things had gotten too far out of hand, and Jubal needed stopping.

Deep in his thoughts, Free worried for Clara and wondered if he had dispatched her to her own death sentence. He figured by insisting she head north on his marked pony, she would draw the attention of White Horse and his raiding party. If she managed that, he felt sure the Kiowa would make a hard run to save him and Parks.

Suddenly jerked from his thoughts, Free threw a pained look to his lower leg. Parks had ranged Horse over, and the mustang's shoulder was pressing into his flesh. He tossed a quick glance to Parks, who was motioning his head to the northeast. Looking left, he caught a glint of sunlight reflecting from the prairie. He followed the reflection across the prairie to a spot below the lower bank of the river. From the underbrush, he saw another flickering of light. *Signals*, he thought. *Maybe she did find them.* Looking back over his shoulder, he yelled.

"Jubal, any reason we can't stop for a drink? You mean to hang us, not have us die of thirst."

"I always figured you for a complainer, Sergeant.

We'll get you some water, all you want, but not till we reach The Flats."

From the corner of his eye, Free saw a Kiowa brave come into view. Appearing from the tall prairie grasses, the lone warrior rode at a slow gait, his gaze straight ahead, as if he was unaware of them.

"Look right," he heard Parks whisper.

Glancing to the south riverbank, he saw another Kiowa brave appear. The brave walked his pony into the shallow riverbed.

For the next few minutes, Free counted as thirty braves emerged from the prairie on both sides of the river. He noticed they never looked toward Jubal. Once all had emerged into view, they followed each other in an extended single file line.

From behind, he heard Jubal exclaim. "What the - !"

"Looks like company, Jubal," Free said.

"Shut-up, Sergeant! Where the hell did they come from?"

"You may have overplayed your hand this time, Sheriff."

"What's that supposed to mean?"

"It means you're riding through Indian Territory alone."

Jubal edged his horse up between Parks and Free, his Colt in hand. "We'll see about that, Sergeant. Put your spurs into those horses. We're going to gallop a little and see what these savages aim to do."

Free touched his pony's flank and watched Parks do the same. Glancing to both sides of the river, he noticed the Kiowa had picked up the same stride and continued to hold their positions on each side of them. The braves kept their stares forward, not once offering any acknowledgement of their prey.

He looked over and could see the sweat beginning to form on Jubal's upper lip. "I don't think they're going anywhere, Sheriff. You might want to take hard consideration about your situation."

"I think these savages just need a little distraction." Jubal holstered his Colt and pulled a thick leather string from behind his saddle.

"What are you talking about, Jubal?

"You boys stay safe and have a nice ride."

Free heard the quirt whoosh through the air, then felt his horse buck and jump to the left. In a flash, the horse was at full gallop, running toward the line of Kiowa. He watched the Indians break formation, turning and riding toward him at full steam. He reckoned they aimed to turn his horse, but with his hands tied, he had no way of helping. Choking the pommel, he held tight as the horse bounded like a wild bronc, splitting the line of Kiowa and sprinting north.

Quick as rabbits, the Kiowa spun and caught back up to him, and soon several braves flanked his horse. One of the braves looped a rawhide string over the horse's head. In an instant, string after string encircled the animal. He felt a violent shaking as the Kiowa pulled back, slowing their ponies and cinching the rawhide strings tight around the runaway's neck. Soon, stopped and unable to shake his captors, Free felt the horse calm.

Relieved, he looked back toward the riverbed to see Parks and Horse circled by a group of Kiowa. Throwing a quick look west, he saw swirls of earth kicked skyward as Jubal tried to flee the Indians. A line of four Kiowa ponies chased after him, gaining ground with each stride.

*   *   *

As one of the braves cut his bindings, Free watched White Horse approaching, Clara in tow. From a distance, the Kiowa chief called.

"Hā chò, "Aungaupi Ch`i!"

"Hā chò, White Horse," he yelled back and raised his right hand, palm out.

"Free!" Clara jumped from her pony and race toward him. "I didn't know if I . . ."

His ropes cut, Free pushed off his mount and ran to meet her. "Shhh . . ." He hugged her, rubbing the back of her neck as a comfort. Glancing up to the Kiowa chief, he smiled. "I owe you for two lives."

"Aungaupi Ch`i, you bring powerful medicine to the prairie, you bring rain when we have none, and soon the buffalo will return. You are a brother to the Kiowa."

Free nodded to the chief. "You are a wise friend."

Turning back to Clara, he held her at arm's length. "Let me look at you."

"Don't worry about me." Parks moved Horse toward the group at a slow canter.

"Parks!"

Grasping Clara's hand, he walked rapidly toward his friend. "I told you we'd get through this."

"I never doubted you, Sergeant."

Free slapped his friend on the shoulder. "I'm glad you're safe." Looking past Parks, he saw in the distance the four Kiowa braves returning; their high-pitched yips, unpleasant and loud, filled the prairie. "I don't think we can say the same for Jubal."

Behind one of the braves, he saw a cloud of dust. Through the powder, he could discern Jubal, tied by string around his neck and hands, desperately trying to keep up with the Indian ponies. Free watched the sheriff run several yards, then stumble to the ground allowing the mustangs to drag him over rock and brush. Struggling to regain his feet, he would right himself for several steps and then stumble to the ground once more. This misery continued for a quarter mile or more.

"Remember what your father said to unjust punishment?" Parks said.

Free bit his lip. "He's done in for sure."

When the four braves rode past, rejoining the rest of their raiding party, Free could see Jubal was a bloody mess. The Kiowa jumped from their ponies, and the entire group began to chatter. Yipping and dancing at the sight of a helpless Jubal, the braves all took turns touching the frightened sheriff with their arrows.

"They're trying to take all of his energy," Parks said. "Leaving him with only fear to fight them."

Free watched the four braves strip the sheriff of his tattered clothing in a concerted frenzy. Several other braves gripped Jubal's arms and legs, encircling each with rawhide. One of the Kiowa, wearing a buffalo head, pushed four broken spears deep into the red sand and began a dance around Jubal. Tied to each lance, the rawhide laces effectively staked Jubal to the prairie.

"We best take our leave," Parks whispered. "There are going to be things that happen here you don't want Clara to carry a memory of."

"Is it wise to depart so soon?" Free looked at Parks, unsure of how to proceed.

"No small talk, remember? You tell the chief,

you need the saddle pack from Jubal's horse. Then you tell him it's time for your medicine to travel east. And Free . . . don't get involved."

Free nodded and walked stiffly toward White Horse. He glanced once more to see the sheriff straddled by one of the braves. The warrior was using an arrowhead to slice his face. Free looked away, sickened by what he witnessed. He had wanted Jubal dead since that day at the arroyo, but now he could only feel the anxious drumming of his heart, not really wishing this fate upon anyone, even Jubal Thompson.

The saddle pack across his shoulder, Free mounted the medicine pony and with a light nudge of his spurs left the Kiowa raiding party at a slow gait.

Strangely silent, he kept his thoughts as they followed the river toward The Flats. Several miles away he turned to Parks and Clara. "No matter his doings, I wanted to stop the Kiowa back there. I couldn't help but feel sympathy for Jubal. Odd, even after all of his trying to kill us, I felt sorry for him."

"That's OK, Free," Parks said. "Feeling sorry for a man has nothing to do with what he may or may not deserve. Sympathy doesn't allow a man to make that distinction."

Free nodded and leaned forward in his saddle. "I reckon we best get this money back to its rightful owners."

"When we do that, I figure old Judge Freemont will have no choice but to clear you of all charges."

Free pointed to the tobacco pouch on Parks' neck and motioned to his mouth. "That oughta make him hotter'n a cathouse on nickel night." Free caught the pouch tossed by Parks.

"Free Anderson!" Clara exclaimed, a grin forming at the corners of her mouth.

Free cut a plug of tobacco and pushed it into his jaw. Pulling the drawstring on the pouch, he tossed it back to Parks.

"You looking for work after all of this?" Parks asked.

"What you got in mind, Lieutenant?" Free bit down on the tobacco plug, sending a thin line of brown to the corners of his mouth.

"I'm looking for a partner."

"You work with Missouri slaves, do you?" Free asked deadpanned.

"Haven't you heard, Sergeant? The slaves are all free."

Free slapped his saddle horn, laughing aloud. "So they are, Lieutenant. So they are."

"And it won't cost you a thing to come aboard. All that's required is a strong back and little need of comfort."

Free stared down the winding riverbank; ahead he envisioned his future. A future with deep roots set in the West Texas soil. He reached over and took Clara's hand, squeezing it firmly. "I've got the woman I love and a friend I can count on, Lieutenant. Everything else is just fuss."

Acknowledgements

I t is very rare that things are accomplished in this world without the help and support of others. My heartfelt thanks go out to:

Weldon L. Edwards, my high school English teacher, who thirty-six years after graduation encouraged me to *finish* the story. Mindy Reed at The Authors' Assistant for her concise editing, guidance, and help along the way. I can honestly say the book might still be sitting on my desk without Mindy's expertise at all things in the writing, publishing realm. Gloria Kempton, whose insights and gentle coaching help bring the writer out in me. Gay Storms for her unique knowledge of West Texas which kept the historical aspects of the manuscript accurate, and also for her profound belief in the project. Fred Tarpley at Word Magic who truly understands the written word and its effect on the reading public. Wanda Reddell, Clarence Holliman, and Charles Scott, three teachers who served as role models for me and many others. Stephanie Barko, literary publicist extraordinaire, who created all ad copy and press releases for media distribution. *The Handbook of Texas Online*, a truly remarkable history resource for all things Texan. The Texas State Historical Association and its partners for making the handbook available to all Texans.

Author's Note

The soldiers of the 62nd Colored Infantry made remarkable sacrifices.

At the Civil War's end, these men and the men of the 65th Colored Infantry began donating money from their pay to found Lincoln Institute, a school where ex-slaves could learn to read and write. The men raised over six-thousand dollars, an astounding accomplishment, when you consider the small sum paid to soldiers during the Civil War. Known today as Lincoln University, the school is home to a campus of diverse students. In May of 2006, the school began seeking donations to help fund a-memorial to the soldiers who made sure that all people had the right to be educated. Information on the Soldier's Memorial fund is located on the following page. It is my hope that all The Road to a Hanging readers will consider a donation. It is a worthwhile cause and the soldier's of the 62nd and 65th certainly deserve the honor.

Soldier's Memorial

The Soldiers' Memorial Plaza is a tribute and a memorial to those enlisted men and officers of the 62nd and 65th Colored Infantries who dreamed of providing an educational institution in Missouri for freed blacks. The Memorial is a permanent status and plaza commemorating the University's founders. These soldiers' small but significant financial contributions provided the funds to establish Lincoln University of Missouri.

An Overview of the Founders and Lincoln University of Missouri

The ex-slaves of the 62nd Colored Infantry were recruited throughout Missouri in 1863 to serve with the Union Forces. They served as "camp laborers" at Baton Rouge, Port Hudson, Mogana, Brazas, and Santiago. Since their enlistments at Benton Barracks in December of 1863, their lives had taken on new meanings. And, it was logical after the War that they would turn their focus on preparing for life.

Two officers especially interested them were Lieutenants Aron M. Adamson and Richard Baxter Foster. Adamson was a native of Nebraska and Foster was from Connecticut, and both had entered the service through the First Nebraska Regiment. They had requested an assignment with Negro troops.

While awaiting orders at Camp McIntosh, Texas, in December 1865, to be mustered out of the service, Adamson asked Foster, whether he would start a school in Missouri, if they were able to raise the money. Adamson started a campaign to raise the money. The proposal caught on quickly and in a short while, most of the men and many of the officers contributed about $4000. Many of the enlisted men who drew $13 a month gave as much as $100, while several officers contributed as much as $200 to the campaign. As the idea spread, some of the members of a neighboring unit, the 65th, took up a similar collection and raised an additional $1,379.

With approximately $6,000 in contributions, Foster and Adamson had in their hand a resolution adopted on January 14, 1866 that laid down the basic foundation for the proposed school:

"Whereas, the freedom of the black race has been achieved by war, and its education is the nest necessity thereof, resolved, that we, the officers and the enlisted men of the 62nd United States Colored Infantry (organized as the First Missouri Volunteers, A.D.). agree to give the sums annexed to our names to aid in founding an educational institution, on the following conditions:

First, the Institute shall be designed for the special benefits of the freed Blacks.

Second, it shall be located in the state of Missouri.

Third, its fundamental idea shall be to combine study with labor, so that the old habits of those who have always labored, but never studied, shall not be thereby changed and that the emancipated slaves, who have neither capital to spend nor time to lose, may obtain an education."

On June 25, 1866, incorporation papers were taken out in the Circuit Court of Cole County, as follows:

State of Missouri, Count of Cole, in vacation, Circuit County Court, Cole County.

Whereas, William Bishop, R. A. Foster, J. Addison Whitaker, Emory S. Foster, Thomas C. Fletcher, R. F. Wingate, Henry Brown, Arnold Krekel, and James E. Yeatman have filed in the office of the Clerk of the Court, the Articles of Association in compliance with the provisions of an act concerning Corporations under the name and style aforesaid, with all power, privileges and immunities granted in act above named

By order of the judge in vacation.

In testimony Whereof, I, William H. Lusk, Clerk of said Court, have here unto set my hand and seal of said Court, done at office in the City of Jefferson, this 25th day of June A. D., 1866.

(Signed) William H. Lusk

Lincoln Institute opened for class on September 14, 1866. with two pupils, Henry Brown and Cornelius Chappelle, but within a few days the building was filled and second teacher was hired. Today, Lincoln University is an 1890 land-grant comprehensive institution that is part of the Missouri state system of higher education. While remaining committed to original purpose, the University has expanded its historical mission to embrace the needs of a significantly broader population reflecting varied social, economic, educational, and cultural backgrounds

The core mission of Lincoln University of Missouri is to provide excellent educational opportunities for a diverse student population in the context of an open enrollment institution . The University provides student-centered learning in a nurturing environment, integrating teaching, research, and service. Lincoln University offers relevant, high quality undergraduate and select graduate programs which students for careers and lifelong learning.

If you would like to make tax-deductible contribution or more information on the Soldiers' Memorial Plaza at Lincoln University, please call (573) 681-5583 or toll free at (800) 836-3707.

Chapter 1

Anderson Homestead, 1868

A harsh wind blew cold on Free Anderson's cheek. Framed against a purple backdrop, gray winter clouds hung low on the northern horizon forming a wall from north to east. The blue norther gushed in during the night plummeting temperatures by forty degrees and reminding man, and beast of the sudden changes that occur on the West Texas plains.

Free stood in the decay of the old Comanche Reservation near the Clear Fork of the Brazos. The numerous structures, abandoned for over a decade, now sat in ruins. On the surrounding prairie, large, rectangular piles of limestone jutted from the ground giving a fort-like appearance to the landscape. Here, at the junction of the southern prairie, and the river woodlands, the fertile plain teemed with deer, wild turkey and water fowl. And it was at this place, that Free staked claim to his homestead.

Free, and Parks looked over the newly constructed three-room house that rose majestically from the prairie. The men had built the structure from the drop logs that once formed the reservation agent's building, and the readily available prairie limestone.

Free wiped his brow, and looked on with pride at their craftsmanship. "I never thought I'd see this day."

"It's a fine home, Free," Parks said, "It's a home in which a man can raise a family."

Turning back to the newly constructed corral, Free placed a loop of string around the corner post, then turned and gave an OK signal to Parks.

The lieutenant secured his end over the opposite corner post and marked the string. "Appears to be square, Free."

Free walked toward his friend, his shoulders pressed hard against his ears. Great puffs of steam exited his mouth with each step. "Gosh, is it cold out here!"

Parks cupped his hands over his mouth and blew heated breath into them. "And by the looks of that cloud bank, this might set with us awhile."

"Well, thank goodness the corral is finished."

"Amen," Parks answered.

"Free! You two best come in and take your breakfast!"

Free glanced toward the backdoor of the newly built wood frame house and saw his mother yelling to them. He waved back an OK to her and looked to Parks, "Let's get out of this cold."

Six months had passed since their final encounter with Jubal. The Old Stone and Dodge ranches had their money returned and in gratitude, the ranchers offered them one thousand dollars each and persuaded Judge Freemont to reconsider his court judgment.

As Free entered his mother's kitchen, childhood smells of coffee and fatback engulfed the room. He pulled a willow chair from the table and invited Parks to sit. Walking toward the iron wood stove, he removed a blackened kettle and poured two cups of coffee. He handed Parks one of the tin cups and sat across from him.

"Who wants eggs?" Martha asked.

Free pressed against the back of his chair and watched his mother set a plate of eggs and fatback in front of him. "Oh that smells wonderful."

"And there are biscuits coming," Clara said.

Free glanced up and watched his bride of five months enter the kitchen. He noticed she was holding a piece of leather with one hand and finishing a stitch with the other.

"All right, Free Anderson," Clara said, "This is for you."

Free accepted the object from Clara and could see it was a tobacco pouch.

"It's about time," Parks laughed.

Free hung the pouch around his neck and then he pointed to Parks, "Can I borrow some of your tobacco to put in here?" Free feigned ignorance as the kitchen erupted in laughter and accusation.

"Free Anderson! You will get your own tobacco!" Clara laughed.

Free pulled an end cut of plug tobacco from his front shirt pocket and held it for the others to observe. "I want everyone to know I bought some yesterday at Dutch Nance's store."

He pushed a fork full of eggs toward his mouth, then smiled as those around him applauded his purchase. He looked toward Parks, and said, "Well you can't say we have occasion for fuss in our lives these days."

The words had no sooner left his mouth than from outside the thunder of buggy wheels rumbled throughout the kitchen. Free threw a surprised glance toward the door.

"What was that you said, Sergeant?"

Free hurried to the kitchen window and saw Murph Jenkins running stiffly toward the house. He rushed to open the door as a rapid series of knocks echoed on the cut cedar.

"What is it, Mr. Jenkins?" Free reached out and pulled the white haired man into the warmth of the kitchen.

"You and Parks need to come quick!"

Rising from his seat, Parks asked, "What is it?"

"It's Samuel! Those mustangs of yours he leased out earlier in the week came back this morning in bad shape. Samuel called the two cowboys on it, and told them they would have to pay a week's worth of keep for how they treated those ponies."

Free sat Mr. Jenkins down in one of the willow chairs and pointed to the stove, "Mother, get him some coffee please." He held the hotel proprietor by the shoulders and asked. "What happened next?"

"They beat him and laughed while they did it. He's gashed deep on his forehead, and he keeps spitting up blood."

"Where is he?" Parks asked.

"He's at the hotel, but the army doc is out at the Wittson Ranch helping Sarah Holder with her baby. Samuel needs some doctoring soon, or I am sure he's gonna die. Those cowboys were mean sorts, all liquored up and playing to the gallery."

Free glanced to Clara and saw she was preparing a bag. "Clara will ride back with you, Mr. Jenkins." He patted the man's arm in reassurance.

"I knew you'd come. Thank you, Clara."

Free watched Parks walk toward Mr. Jenkins.

"And those cowboys, where are they?"

"The both of them are in Kelley's drinking."

The Flats lay eight miles to the south of Free's homestead. Following the Clear Fork, both men rode silent in the cold until Fort Griffin came into view.

"What are you aiming to do, Parks?"

"I reckon if these boys are roostered enough to beat a helpless man like Samuel, not much good is fixing to come out of this."

"Likely so," Free said. He pulled his Colt from its holster and checked his ammo.

"It would be nice if the county could find a new sheriff," Parks said.

"You and I both know they aren't going to get anyone to take the job. They won't pay near enough for a man with any sense to risk his neck sheriffing The Flats." Free slid the Colt back in its cover.

"Especially when they know we're dumb enough to do it for free."

Parks tied Horse to the hitching post in front of Kelley's. He stepped onto the boardwalk with a careful look in each direction. He needed to make sure he and Free entered the saloon without a surprise from their backs. To the west, he saw Milt Davies walking toward him, waving his hand in the air.

"Parks!" The man hollered.

Parks stopped on the boardwalk and waited for the Kelley's regular to make his way to him and Free.

"Parks, thank goodness you two are here," Milt said. "There are two hard cases in the bar. They're the ones who gave Samuel a beating this morning and now they've run everyone out of the bar. They need dealing with before they kill someone."

"They the only two in the bar, Milt?" Parks kept his gaze on the saloon doors.

"Yep. One of them is tall and heavyset; he's the one who beat Samuel."

"OK. thanks, Milt, you just go on about your business and Free and I will take care of this."

Parks watched Milt walk back west and then looked at Free. "I'm going in first and see where these boys are situated. You give me a minute and then come in and set yourself on the opposite side of the bar from them."

"Be careful, Lieutenant."

Inside the bar, Parks noticed the two cowboys standing off to the left, in front of the Faro and Chuck-a-Luck tables. Both had a good view of the swinging doors and anyone who tried to enter the saloon. He walked to the middle of the bar and surveyed the room. Mr. Kelley ran a dirty rag in and out of a glass, nodded at his approach then slightly titled his head toward the cowboys.

"What'll it be, Parks?"

"Tobacco." Parks placed both his hands on the bar.

Parks watched as Kelley set a wooden bowl on the counter filled with tobacco. He cut a plug off one of the ends and nodded back to the owner.

"The bar's closed right now, cowboy."

Parks swung a hard gaze over to the pair. He looked at the taller of the two, the one doing the talking. "You must be the cowboy who spent all week breaking down my ponies." Parks spit brown liquid toward the cuspidor at his feet.

"Oh those were your nags; well I guess we beat the wrong man then." The heavyset cowboy laughed.

Hearing the squeaky hinges of the saloon door creak, Parks glanced up to the bar mirror and saw Free walk inside. He turned his gaze to the cowboys and noticed the talker toss back a shot of whiskey.

"Ain't this nice, they let coloreds drink with white folks in this burg."

Free moved to the east end of the bar and leaned on the wooden counter staring across to the cowboys.

"Morning, Free."

"Morning, Mr. Kelley."

Parks spit once more and then he glanced toward the end of the bar. With hands clenched in tight fists and his back set straight, he proceeded point-blank for the talker.

"You might want to watch yourself, horse peddler. I don't take kindly to a man getting too close to me." The cowboy moved his right hand below the bar in a slow deliberate motion.

Keeping his eyes locked on the cowboy, Parks rounded the corner of the bar with hard purpose. Face to face with the man, he saw the cowboy's hand wrapped around an ivory pistol handle.

"You've got some moxie. . . ." The man uttered.

In one quick motion, Parks' left hand surrounded the cowboy's pistol grip and using his strength, he held the man's Colt in its holster.

"Arrrg." He heard the cowboy groan as his knuckles cracked against metal.

With lightning speed, Parks pulled his Colt and thrust the barrel against the cowboy's cheekbone while releasing his grip from the man's pistol. "Go ahead and pull that Colt, cowboy! Let's see how you back up your wind!"

"And you!" Free barked across the bar to the man's companion. "Set your hands on the bar!"

Parks made sure the cowboy's companion moved his hands onto the bar as ordered and then he looked back to the talker. Forcing his Colt deeper into the cowboy's cheek, he said, "Now big talker, I believe you owe Samuel twenty-five dollars for his injuries and you owe me another eight dollars for the horses."

"You're gonna regret this, horseman. You better kill me now cause I'll come back looking for you after we're done here today!"

Parks felt a surge of energy gush through his chest. Without a thought, he raised his left hand and whacked the cowboy hard across the mouth. He watched the man dip and then wipe his mouth with the back of his hand, a trickle of blood visible on the corner of his mouth. "You're not dealing with an old livery owner now cowboy!" Parks saw a darkness cloud the cowboy's eyes and he figured this affair could only end one way. "Now, you reach deep into your pocket, cowboy and pull out some dollars. If you don't have any, you and your friend are gonna spend considerable time in the jail! Understand?"

With angry reluctance, the cowboy thrust a hand into his pocket and pulled out a roll of cash, his face flushed scarlet as he slapped his money on the bar.

Parks looked to Kelley and said, "Count out

thirty-three dollars from his roll and hang onto it for me."

Kelley moved toward them, counted out the money and then set the cowboy's roll back on the bar.

"Now cowboy, pick up the rest of your money and you and your friend get out of here! And from now on, you best ride clear of The Flats! The next time I see you I won't be as friendly!"

Parks removed his gun from the man's cheek, but he kept it in full view for both men to see. He watched as both men ambled slowly out of the bar and held his Colt steady at the swinging doors as they exited. As the doors swung back and forth, Parks motioned with his Colt for Free to get down and then moving right, he braced his shoulder against the inside wall of the saloon.

As the doors quieted, the talker burst back inside, his gun drawn, spraying lead toward the west corner of the bar filling the room with smoke.

"I knew you were too stupid to leave with breath in your lungs cowboy!" Parks' Colt roared, sending the cowboy back through the swinging doors.

Parks looked over to Free as he rose from behind the bar. "Hey, cowboy number two!" He yelled to the street. "When I walk out these doors if I see a pistol in your hands, I will shoot you as dead as your friend!"

Parks held for an instant and then heard the jingle of spurs on the boardwalk hightailing it away. He pushed through the swinging doors and saw the talker lying on his back in the street, then glanced west. He saw the cowboy's companion hurrying toward Fort Griffin.

"This one's dead," Free said.

"You know this fella, Kelley?" Parks asked. "I know that Samuel leased him horses to ride to Fort Concho, but he didn't give me any names."

"I know of him," Kelley answered. "Parks, that's Tig Hardy's younger brother, Chase."

"Who's Tig Hardy?" Free asked.

Kelley kicked at the body with his boot, as if to guarantee he was dead before he answered. "He's the man who bushwhacked those three soldiers of the 10th Cavalry outside of Fort Concho. Story goes he killed all three and then cut off their chevrons. He's a detestable character who's been sitting in the jail at the Fort awaiting trial."

"You think this cowboy and his friend rode our mustangs the eighty miles to Fort Concho?"

Parks looked toward the stage depot and tightened his jaw. "Would appear so and my gut's telling me Tig Hardy is no longer sitting in jail."

Parks looked over to Kelley, who was still sizing up the younger Hardy's body. "What do you think Tig's gonna do when he learns his brother is dead?"

"I suspect, he's gonna come looking for the man who done his brother in."

"I reckon that's so." Parks stared grimly at the corpse. "Free, why don't you check on Samuel, and Kelley and I will get this body moved off the street."

MEDICINE ROAD

WILL HENRY

Mountain man Jim Bridger is counting on Jesse Callahan. He knows that Callahan is the best man to lead the wagon train that's delivering guns and ammunition to Bridger's trading post at Green River. But Brigham Young has sworn to wipe out Bridger's posts, and he's hired Arapahoe warrior Watonga to capture those weapons at any cost. Bridger, Young and Watonga all have big plans for those guns, but it's all going to come down to just how tough Callahan can be. He's going to have to be tougher than leather if he hopes to make it to the post...alive.

ISBN 10: 0-8439-5814-6
ISBN 13: 978-0-8439-5814-0

NIGHT HAWK
STEPHEN OVERHOLSER

He came to the ranch with a mile-wide chip on his shoulder and no experience whatsoever. But it was either work on the Circle L or rot in jail, and he figured even the toughest labor was better than a life behind bars. He's got a lot to learn though, and he'd better learn it fast because he's about to face one of the toughest cattle drives in the country. They've got an ornery herd, not much water and danger everywhere they look. The greenhorn the cowboys call Night Hawk may not know much, but he does know this: The smallest mistake could cost him his life.

ISBN 10: 0-8439-5840-5
ISBN 13: 978-0-8439-5840-9

HEADING WEST
Western Stories
NOEL M. LOOMIS

Noel M. Loomis creates characters so real it's hard to believe they're fiction, and these nine stories vividly demonstrate his brilliant storytelling talent. Within this volume, you'll meet Big Blue Buckley, who proves it takes a "Tough *Hombre*" to build a railroad in the 1880s and "The St. Louis Salesman" who struggles with the harsh terrain of the Texas prairie. Most poignant of all is the dying Comanche warrior passing on the ways of his people in "Grandfather Out of the Past," a tale that won Loomis the prestigious Spur Award. Each story sweeps you back in time to the Old West as it really was.

ISBN 10: 0-8439-5897-9
ISBN 13: 978-0-8439-5897-3

LOUIS L'AMOUR
Grub Line Rider

Louis L'Amour is one of the most popular and honored authors of the past hundred years. Millions of readers have thrilled to his tales of courage and adventure, tales that have transported them to the Old West and brought to life that exciting era of American history. Here, collected together in paperback for the first time, are seven of L'Amour's finest stories, all carefully restored to their original magazine publication versions.

Whether he's writing about a cattle town in Montana ("Black Rock Coffin Makers"), a posse pursuit across the desert ("Desert Death Song"), a young gunfighter ("Ride, You Tonto Riders"), or a violent battle to defend a homestead ("Grub Line Rider"), L'Amour's powerful presentation of the American West is always vibrant and compelling. This volume represents a golden opportunity to experience these stories as Louis L'Amour originally intended them to be read.

AVAILABLE MARCH 2008!

ISBN 13: 978-0-8439-6065-5

MAX BRAND®

Luck

Pierre Ryder is not your average Jesuit missionary. He's able to ride the meanest horse, run for miles without tiring, and put a bullet in just about any target. But now he's on a mission of vengeance to find the man who killed his father. The journey will test his endurance to its utmost—and so will the extraordinary woman he meets along the way. Jacqueline "Jack" Boone has all the curves of a lady but can shoot better than most men. In the epic tradition of *Riders of the Purple Sage*, their story is one for the ages.

AVAILABLE MARCH 2008!

ISBN 13: 978-0-8439-5875-1

The Bloody Texans

Kent Conwell

Trapper and scout Nathan Cooper returned home to his cabin in East Texas, only to find a sight he would never forget—his wife, his young niece and his niece's intended, all slaughtered. With his heart broken and blood in his eyes, Nathan buried his family in the cold ground. Then he made an oath. He swore that the men who did this would pay. Nathan would use all of his skills to hunt the murdering scum, and he would see them suffer. One by one, he will track them and kill them, even if he has to break down the gates of Hell to do it!

AVAILABLE APRIL 2008!

ISBN 13: 978-0-8439-6066-2

LOREN ZANE GREY

continues in the grand tradition of his father,

Zane Grey,®

with the further adventures of Lassiter—
the rough-riding hero from
RIDERS OF THE PURPLE SAGE
who became one of the
greatest Western legends of all time.

LONE GUN

When Lassiter promises to protect his dead friend's son, he never thinks the young rancher will run into such a passel of trouble. Yet before he knows it, there's an all-out range war led by a pack of hired sharpshooters trying to steal the kid's land—and their lives. They figure that one man can't last long, but they haven't reckoned on...

THE LASSITER LUCK

AVAILABLE APRIL 2008!

ISBN 13: 978-0-8439-5815-7